Based on the Motion Picture

Story by George Lucas
Screenplay by Bob Dolman
Adaptation by Joan D. Vinge

Random House 🏠 New York

Library of Congress Cataloging-in-Publication Data:

Vinge, Joan D. Willow : based on the motion picture. SUMMARY: In a magical land, a poor farmer is entrusted with the care of an infant destined to become a good and wise queen and bring about the downfall of the evil sorceress who is the present queen. [1. Fantasy] I. Lucas, George. II. Dolman, Bob. III. Willow (Motion picture : 1988) IV. Title. PZ7.V7457Wi 1988 [Fic] 88-4590 ISBN: 0-394-89573-8 (pbk.); 0-394-99573-2 (lib. bdg.)

Manufactured in the United States of America 1 2 3 4 5 6 7 8 9 0

One

Vultures wheeled above the bleak mountainside. They were hungry, as they always were. But even they avoided Nockmaar Castle, the dark fortress that crouched on the sheer black cliffs. No one ever visited Nockmaar Castle by choice.

A scream echoed through the castle's brooding halls. It did not come from the torture chambers this time, but from a cell deep in the dungeons, where six pregnant women were imprisoned. One of them was giving birth to her child.

Sorsha, the red-haired daughter of Nockmaar's queen, watched and frowned as Ethna, the midwife, lifted the baby up. "Is it a girl?" she asked.

"Yes," Ethna answered.

"Show me its arms," Sorsha said.

Ethna held out the newborn's tiny arms. On the baby's right arm was a small, oddly shaped mark. "It bears the mark," she murmured.

Sorsha peered at the crying baby, then turned away. "The prophecy has come true. I must tell my mother." She hurried out of the cell.

3

Gently and sadly Ethna wrapped the baby in clean rags and handed her to her mother. The woman clutched the baby and looked up at Ethna desperately. "Ethna, please. Help me," she whispered. "They're going to kill her."

Ethna, frightened, glanced at the guards outside the cell. "Queen Bavmorda will kill you if you try to stop her," she said. Bavmorda already ruled the land with cruelty and sorcery. Soon her powers would spread through the entire world. But she had learned of a prophecy: that a special child with a birthmark on its arm would somehow keep her from her goal, unless it was destroyed.

"Save my baby!" the woman begged. "Take her far away . . . please!"

Ethna looked into her eyes. This woman was willing to give up her life to save her child—to save their world. How could she herself do any less? Quickly she bundled some rags into the shape of a baby and handed them to the woman.

"Ethna . . . thank you," the woman murmured. Her eyes shone. She kissed her baby and passed it to Ethna, who hid it in her basket of rags. Trembling with fear, Ethna hurried out of the dungeon, cringing as Queen Bavmorda swept by her.

Queen Bavmorda entered the cell. "So. You *were* the one," she said, glaring down at the woman.

The young mother raised her head. "You cannot change the prophecy," she said defiantly.

"This child will have no power over me," snapped Bavmorda, reaching for the bundle the woman held in her arms. She tore the rags aside but found nothing in them. "Where is the baby?" she cried.

"The midwife!" Sorsha exclaimed, looking over her

shoulder.

"Find that baby, Sorsha!" Bavmorda snarled. "Use the dogs! Bring her back to me alive!"

"My daughter will destroy you, Bavmorda!" the young mother cried. "Your reign of terror is at an end! You can't stop her!"

Sorsha ran up the stairs, with two guards following behind her.

Bavmorda glowered at the baby's mother and turned to the waiting guards. "Kill her," she snarled.

Sorsha called out the queen's brutal troops and set the monstrous Death Dogs on the trail. They followed the fleeing midwife across the land. But for months Ethna escaped them, through luck and her own courage.

Then one morning, in a hiding place she had hoped the queen's minions would never find, Ethna woke to hear the hideous baying of the Death Dogs. Clutching the baby, she ran down to the riverbank, where she tore loose a mat of reeds and made a makeshift boat. She put the baby in it and sent it swirling away downstream. Then she ran across the shallow river, drawing the dogs after her.

The snarling dogs caught up with her as she tried to climb the steep riverbank. She beat at them futilely with a stick, knowing as she fell back that nothing could save her. But she knew too, as the baby drifted out of sight, that she had done the right thing.

TWO

Laughter filled the air as two very small children played on the quiet riverbank. Poking their heads through the reeds in a search for frogs, Ranon Ufgood and his little sister, Mims, stopped suddenly in amazement. There before them was a baby, lying on a makeshift raft. Ranon jumped to his feet and ran up the hill, calling, "Dada! Dada!" His sister followed as fast as she could.

Up in the field above, their father, Willow Ufgood, halted his enormous plow hog. Willow was hardly more than a boy himself, for his people married young. He wished he could be down by the stream too, instead of up here plowing and planting. He reached into his sack for another handful of seeds.

"Dada!" Ranon shouted. "We found something in the river!"

Willow smiled fondly at his children. "I can't run off and play with you now, Ranon. I've got work to do."

"But Dada," Ranon and Mims chimed together, "you've got to see it! Hurry!"

6

The hog glared disapprovingly as Willow gave in. He followed his children down the hill.

Willow gaped at the sight that was waiting for him: a baby caught in the weeds. A *big* baby. Mims was trying to pull its raft to shore. "Mims! Back!" he, ordered. "Don't go near it. We don't know where it's been. It could be diseased!"

She looked up at him, wide-eyed. "But Dada, it's a baby."

"It's not like us," Ranon said, realizing suddenly how large it really was.

"No," Willow agreed, "it's not a Nelwyn; it's too big. It looks like a Daikini baby." Most Nelwyns never grew to more than three or four feet tall. This infant was half that long already.

"What's a Daikini?" Ranon asked.

"Daikinis are giants who live far away," Willow said brusquely. The peace-loving Nelwyns preferred to have nothing to do with the Daikinis and their endless wars.

The baby smiled at him.

"Ooh, she's so cute. . . ." Mims cooed, reaching out again.

"Mims! Careful!" Willow snapped. "It might bite." He pulled her back. The baby began to cry.

"Can't we keep it, Dada?" Ranon asked.

"Absolutely not," said Willow. "We'll push it downstream and forget we ever saw it."

"Ufgood! Willow Ufgood!"

Willow leaped up in a panic when he heard the braying voice of Burglekutt, the village prefect. "Shh!" he hissed. "It's the prefect. That's all I need. Keep quiet. Don't touch it." He repeated the age-old, useless parental warning as he rushed back up

7

the hill to answer the summons.

As he reached the plow he saw Burglekutt coming across his field, chased by Kiaya, Willow's wife. The sight of his wife's long, beautiful hair shining in the sunlight made Willow smile in spite of himself. The smile disappeared as Burglekutt reached him.

"Mr. Burglekutt!" Kiaya cried. "My husband hasn't stolen anything!"

Burglekutt scooped a handful of seeds out of Willow's sack and waved them furiously. "Ufgood! You still haven't paid your debts to me. Where did you get these seeds?"

Willow pushed his hand away. "Maybe I used my magic," he said, daring to be impertinent because Burglekutt had dared to upset his wife.

"You're no sorcerer, Ufgood," Burglekutt snarled. "You're a clown. I sell the planting seeds around here. Now tell me where you got these."

Willow put his arm around his wife. "My family's been gathering them in the forest since last fall. There's no law against that, Mr. Burglekutt." As he finished speaking, he heard the children laugh down by the river.

Kiaya stiffened. "Where are the children? Willow, you didn't leave them alone by the river?" She pulled away and ran toward the riverbank.

Willow nervously watched her go. He looked back when Burglekutt sneered, "Magic! You'll need magic if you expect to get your planting done before the rains start." He flung the seed at Willow's feet and grabbed him by the collar. "I will have this land, Ufgood," he threatened, "and you will end up working in the mines." He let Willow go, turned away—and walked directly into the side of Willow's hog. The hog grunted indignantly and butted him backward into the mud.

Willow retreated with great haste.

Down by the river he found Kiaya—just as he had feared, with the Daikini baby in her arms.

"Oh, Willow. . . ." Kiaya murmured, smiling down at the baby.

"Kiaya," Willow gasped, "absolutely under no condition is anyone in this family going to fall in love with that baby."

The baby laughed, and everyone fell in love. Kiaya carried her away up the bank with the children trailing after her, as if Willow had ceased to exist.

"Hey! I will not be ignored!" Willow shouted futilely, and followed them back across the fields.

Inside their small cottage Willow paced anxiously while Kiaya poured water into a wooden tub. "This is terrible, Kiaya," he said. "If we're caught with her, it will be the end of us. What are we going to do?"

"We're going to give her a bath," Kiaya said calmly. "Now don't be such a ninny-goat." She settled the baby into the bathtub, smiling as the infant giggled.

"Isn't she cute?" Mims danced around them. "Look at her toes."

Ranon, trying to pretend that he wasn't impressed, poked among his father's magic props, picking up colored feathers and pieces of bright cloth.

"Careful with that, Ranon," Willow admonished. "I need it for the festival tomorrow."

Kiaya washed the baby gently, stopping a moment to look at the odd birthmark on her arm. "Willow, do you think we should take her to the Village Council?"

"No!" Willow said, aghast. "They'll think it's a bad omen! There'll be a flood or a drought and they'll blame me for it!" He began to pace again, waving his arms. " 'Ufgood brought around that Daikini, didn't he?' 'That's right, and he's a lousy farmer, too.' 'Let's get him!' "

"Willow, calm down," Kiaya murmured. Willow was always a worrier, but today he seemed more easily upset than usual.

"Calm down? Kiaya!" he shouted. "Tomorrow's my big day! I'm about to become apprentice to the High Aldwin!"

So that was what was making him so nervous. Her husband was not only a worrier, he was a dreamer as well. She sighed. "Love," she said patiently, "the High Aldwin hasn't picked a new apprentice in years."

"Tomorrow's going to be different," Willow insisted. "He's going to pick me. And this little baby's not going to ruin it."

The baby began to cry as Kiaya lifted her from the bath and wrapped her in a towel. Kiaya held the infant out to Willow.

"Hey," he protested. "I don't want her, Kiaya."

"Hold her while I get some milk." She dropped the howling baby into his arms and turned away.

The moment he took the baby, she stopped crying.

"She likes you, Dada," Ranon said.

Willow squinted at the baby. She smiled. Reluctantly, he smiled back.

Three

Music and celebration filled the flower-strewn streets as the Nelwyn townfolk danced and sang. The Spring Festival was the high point of their year, and all the people joined in, putting on their best clothes and best entertainments. Miners battled farmers in a tug of war while the crowd cheered; musicians played; craftspeople sold their wares; children laughed and shouted. Burglekutt and the five other members of the Village Council sat watching on a high platform, mildly amused.

Willow had been preparing all year for this day. Standing on a stage he did magic trick after magic trick, hoping to win the High Aldwin's approval. He listened and smiled as the sparse audience applauded when he made feathers appear out of nowhere. At last, ready for his grand finale, he called out, "And now! For my final amazing feat I will make an entire pig disappear!"

His best friend, Meegosh, who always cheered the most, applauded louder as Mims and Ranon dragged a baby pig onto the stage. Willow took it, and it bit his hand. The crowd laughed, and half of them started away, shaking their heads. Meegosh covered his face.

Determinedly Willow waved his cloak. "Whuppity bairn, deru, deru!" he cried.

The pig disappeared. The crowd gasped, and the doubters turned back again.

With an indignant squeal the piglet wriggled out of a hidden pocket in Willow's cloak, dashed through his legs, and leaped off the stage to a loud chorus of booing.

Willow gathered up his magic props forlornly, his face red with embarrassment, as the crowd flowed away.

Meegosh climbed onto the stage, carrying the piglet. "That was excellent, Willow!" Meegosh said, trying to lift his friend's spirits. "A lot better than last year. You need a better pig, that's all." They began to walk through the festival together. As they passed the Village Council, Burglekutt sneered down at Willow. "Don't worry about Burglekutt," Meegosh said. "Once you're the High Aldwin's apprentice, Burglekutt will grovel at your feet." He put an arm around his friend as they wandered on into the crowd.

Later in the day, Willow joined the two other would-be apprentice magicians as the High Aldwin mounted his platform.

"Attention!" a councilman called. "The High Aldwin will now make his choice for a new apprentice! Bring forth the hopefuls!" Excitement ran through the crowd as Willow and the other candidates came forward.

"Willow Ufgood?" Burglekutt called loudly. "A hopeful? How'd *he* get picked? Is this a joke?" He howled with laughter, urging his fellow councilmen to join in.

The High Aldwin silenced them with a look, then turned to address the three hopefuls. "Magic is the bloodstream of the universe," he said. "Forget all you know or think you know. All that you require is your intuition. The power to control the world is in which finger?" He held up four fingers. The first two candidates each picked a finger quickly, and the High Aldwin shook his head each time. Willow hesitated, biting his lip. He glanced up at the High Aldwin and saw anticipation and encouragement in the old wizard's eyes. He opened his mouth to speak—closed it, and picked one of the remaining fingers. Disappointment showed on the High Aldwin's face. He shook his head and pounded the ground with his staff. "No apprentice this year!" he announced.

Burglekutt brayed with laughter, and the crowd broke into a chaos of shouting.

Willow looked down, his shoulders drooping. But there was still something preying on his mind . . . the baby. He had to tell the High Aldwin about it, no matter how difficult that seemed right now. "Sir!" he called. "I have to talk to you! It's a matter of great importance."

"You had your chance, Ufgood," Burglekutt snapped. "Now back away! I have a meeting—"

Suddenly a shriek of terror tore through the festival sounds. Music and laughter stopped everywhere as parents grabbed their children and ran for their lives. A Death Dog ripped through the village, ransacking huts, dragging out cribs and cradles. It knocked down a garland-covered stand, destroying it, and charged down the street toward Willow and Ranon.

"Mims! Mims!" Willow shouted as he realized that his little daughter was nowhere in sight. Then he saw her standing frozen with fear right in the Death Dog's path. Frantically he ran toward her, snatched her up, and carried her out of its way.

A loud war cry stopped the dog in its tracks. Vohnkar, the village's head warrior, led a crowd of armed miners and farmers down the street. They surrounded the Death Dog and attacked it with shovels and picks. At last Vohnkar and two of his best men drove their spears through the dog's chest. It died with a howl that stood their hair on end.

Slowly the other villagers returned to the square. They looked around, stunned. One man picked up a broken cradle. "It was looking for somebody's baby!" he said with a shudder. The villagers gathered around the garland-covered stand, the symbol of the festival and of their peaceful way of life. It was smashed now almost beyond recognition. Everyone was silent.

Willow, realizing that he alone knew what baby the dog had been searching for, looked on with unspoken guilt. Mims clung to his hand, her eyes still wide with fear. "Mommy?" she asked in a small voice. With a sudden sinking terror Willow grabbed his children's hands and ran toward his home.

Willow found Kiaya standing peacefully by the window, feeding the baby. He threw his arms around her and hugged her close. Stepping back again, he looked down into the baby's smiling face. Kiaya stared at him with surprise and concern.

"We can't keep her, Kiaya," he said softly. "We have to take her to the Council." Kiaya didn't argue, sensing from his manner that something was terribly wrong. Mims and Ranon came in through the door behind him. They all clung together for a long moment, cherishing their precious lives and each other.

They could hear the villagers arguing long before they reached the door of the Council building. The Council sat on a platform at the front of the room, with the High Aldwin in his special seat above them.

Burglekutt pounded the floor with his stick. "Silence!" he cried. "One beast we can kill. But there may be more. And they won't give up till they've found what they're looking for!"

Holding the baby, Willow tried to push his way through the jostling crowd.

"It's a sign!" someone yelled.

"There'll be a drought! Or a plague!" someone else shouted. "Our village will be destroyed!"

"Who's to blame for this?" Others began to join in the shouting. "Let's find the culprit and throw him in the pit!"

Willow stopped as the words registered. He turned around and started back toward the door. But the High Aldwin, looking out over the crowd, raised a hand and pointed. "Willow Ufgood!" he called. Willow froze. "Come forward."

The crowd parted. Willow walked the length of the room and stood before him. Kiaya and the children followed partway, stopping next to Meegosh.

"Earlier today you tried to tell me something, Willow," the High Aldwin said.

Willow bowed his head. "My children found this baby in the river, High Aldwin."

The crowd began to stir. The High Aldwin silenced them with a gesture. He placed his hand on the baby's head. "A Daikini child. . . ." he murmured. "I feel . . ."

"That's what the beasts want!" Burglekutt shouted. "Let's give it to them!" The people in the crowd muttered again, most of them agreeing.

"But they'll kill her," Willow protested. "You can't!"

"It isn't one of us!" Burglekutt cried, whipping up the crowd's anger.

The High Aldwin ignored their shouting. He seemed to be in a trance as he stood over the child. "Yes . . ." he said, "this child . . . is special. . . ." He opened his eyes. The room fell silent, waiting for his decision. "This child must be taken beyond the boundaries of our village. All the way across the great river to the Daikini crossroads."

A chill ran through the crowd. Their cries were filled with panic now. "Who will do that?" someone demanded.

"It seems only fair that the man to take this baby to the crossroads be the very man who plucked it out of the river," Burglekutt shouted. "I nominate Willow Ufgood!" He pointed at Willow. The crowd yelled wildly.

"No, wait, I can't go!" Willow protested. "I haven't put my crop in yet!"

The High Aldwin studied the crowd. He stepped forward, rattling something in his cupped hands. "I will consult the bones!" he called. He scattered a handful of small animal bones across the floor between himself and Willow. As he leaned over, seeming to study them, he whispered to Willow, "The bones tell me nothing. But I must make a decision.

Do you have any love for this child?"

Willow stared at the High Aldwin in stunned disbelief. Then he looked down at the baby, into her innocent eyes that gazed up at him with such trust. "Yes . . ." he whispered, "yes, I do."

The High Aldwin straightened up and called out, "The bones have spoken!" He gestured. "Willow? The security of this village depends on you!" Willow nodded numbly.

"Praise the bones!" Burglekutt cheered. The crowd cheered with him.

"But you will need help," the High Aldwin said. "The outer world is a dangerous and corrupt place, and this baby is hunted by bloodthirsty beasts. Now I ask all of you: Who has the courage to protect our brave fellow on his journey?"

Vohnkar elbowed his way forward, accompanied by two strong warriors. "I'll go!" he said.

"Vohnkar! Vohnkar!" the crowd shouted.

"Not Vohnkar," Burglekutt protested. "He's the best warrior in the village. What if the beasts return? We need him here."

"He must stay! Vohnkar must stay!" the crowd echoed.

Vohnkar and his men stepped back again.

"What are you thinking of?" Kiaya cried, appalled. "Willow can't go alone!" The villagers around her glanced at one another guiltily, but no one volunteered. At last Meegosh stepped forward. "I'll go with him."

"Good!" Burglekutt said, delighted to be rid of his two least favorite people. "Excellent choice! Praise the bones!"

The High Aldwin glanced at Burglekutt, annoyed.

"Now all this expedition needs is a leader," he said, "and according to the bones, that leader is . . . you, Burglekutt."

The grin vanished from Burglekutt's face. He bent down, frowning at the bones. He looked up at the High Aldwin, who nodded solemnly. Burglekutt gazed out over the crowd. "Vohnkar!" he shouted.

Early the next morning Willow, Meegosh, and Burglekutt gathered with Vohnkar and two of his warriors by the looming druid stones on Sacred Hill. Somberly they packed up their supplies and said good-bye to their families. Kiaya, her long golden hair covered with a kerchief, cradled the baby for the last time. Willow looked out over the distant, fog-shrouded forest.

Mims clung to his hand. "Are you scared, Dada?" she asked.

"No," Willow said, as nonchalantly as he could.

"Even with fairies in the woodland that'll put you to sleep for a hundred years?" Ranon asked, impressed.

"Doesn't bother me," Willow murmured.

"Brownies?" Ranon said.

"Dragons?" Mims echoed.

"Trolls!" Ranon exclaimed. "Trolls that'll skin you alive and take your face and—"

"Ranon!" Willow yelled. He took a deep breath. "You know I hate trolls. . . ."

"I could be your guard!" Ranon cried eagerly. "I could carry your spear!"

"Me too!" Mims squealed. "Me too!"

Willow smiled, hugging his children close. "What a lucky father I am. I wish I could take you bobbins with me." He leaned down and whispered, "Take good care of your mother and don't let her worry about me. I'll be fine." He kissed each of them and straightened up again. Meegosh's doting mother was still fussing over him. Willow stood silently as Kiaya put the baby into the pack he wore.

"We've never been apart," said Kiaya. "I miss you already."

"Don't worry, Kiaya," said Willow, trying to reassure himself as well. "I'll be back before you know it."

Kiaya kissed the baby and looked into her husband's eyes. "Remember to keep her warm. Here. This will bring you luck." She pressed something into his hand: a braid of her hair.

"You cut your hair?" Willow said, incredulous, looking at her scarf-covered head. *Her beautiful hair.* He kissed her with love and gratitude.

"Good, brave people!" the High Aldwin called. "The outer world is no place for a Nelwyn. Give the baby to the first Daikini you see, then hurry home." The small band of travelers stood together as the High Aldwin held up a stone and chanted, "Tuatha . . . lokwatthrak . . . tuatha!" He flung the rock into the air. Before their startled eyes it changed into a bird. "Go in the direction the bird is flying," he cried.

The travelers watched in confusion as the bird circled in the air and flew back toward the village. "It's going back to the village," Burglekutt said.

The High Aldwin scratched his head. "Ignore the bird," he said irritably. "Follow the river."

"All right, men," Burglekutt said, clapping his hands.

"Move out!" Vohnkar ordered, ignoring Burglekutt.

As the others started down the hill, the High Aldwin caught Willow's shoulder and drew him aside. "What's your problem, son?" he whispered.

"How do you mean?" Willow asked, puzzled.

The High Aldwin looked impatient. "When I held up my fingers, what was your first impulse?"

Willow looked at his feet, embarrassed. "It was stupid. . . ." he mumbled.

The High Aldwin gave him a shake. "Just tell me!"

"To choose my own finger," Willow said.

The High Aldwin nodded, satisfied. "You lack faith in yourself, Willow," he said gently. He pulled out a small flask of mead. "Drink?"

"No." Willow shook his head, still trying to believe that his instinct had actually been right.

The High Aldwin took a quick swig and put the flask away. "More than anyone in this village," he said, "you have the potential to be a great sorcerer." Willow stared at him, even more surprised. "When you get out there, listen to your own heart. You must learn to trust your intuition. Now, here. These will protect you." He dropped three small objects into Willow's hand.

"Acorns?" Willow asked dubiously.

"They're magical," the High Aldwin said, growing impatient again. "Anything you hurl them at will turn to stone."

"Ufgood!" Burglekutt bellowed from halfway down the hill. "Hurry up, you lazy lout!"

"I'd love to throw one at Burglekutt," Willow muttered.

"I know how you feel," the High Aldwin said. "But if you use sorcery for evil, you will become evil.

You have much to learn, young Ufgood." He patted Willow's shoulder, smiling in farewell.

Willow smiled back and started after the others.

"Willow!" Kiaya called. She ran after him down the hill and threw herself into his arms, kissing him passionately, with tears in her eyes. She let him go again, looking one last time at the baby. "Don't let anything happen to her," she said.

Willow nodded, too full of feeling for words. He adjusted the baby's pack on his back, waved to his children, and set out after his companions on the longest journey of his life.

Four

The Nelwyn travelers hiked through strange and wonder-filled terrain all day. None of them had ever been so far from home or even dreamed of the kinds of things they saw now. But Willow and Meegosh, loaded down like pack mules under their burdens of supplies, found it hard to appreciate the constantly changing view.

Willow struggled to feed the baby as he trudged along, scowling at Burglekutt's wide back. Burglekutt strode along, carrying nothing but a walking stick, and never stopped to rest because *he* was never tired. "I hate this," Willow muttered. The baby began to cry.

Vohnkar and his men shook their spears at an enormous beast that loomed unexpectedly in front of them—the first bear they had ever seen. It shambled away into the trees, as startled as they were by the intrusion. The travelers went on again.

After a few steps Willow slowed. "We have to stop," he called.

"Stop?" Vohnkar said. "Why?"

"The baby's sick."

"She's not sick," Burglekutt said impatiently. "Let me see—" He took the baby out of Willow's pack. The baby threw up on him.

Meegosh pressed his hands to his head. "Oh, no!" he cried. "Is she going to die?"

"She'll be fine if she gets some rest." Willow took the baby back from Burglekutt. This time there were no arguments.

The Nelwyns camped for the night. They roasted a fish, sitting close together on a log by the fire because of the chill in the air. Meegosh played his flute while Willow wiped the baby's feverish face and sang her a lullaby. He held her close, stroking her downy hair, and whispered, "You're feeling better, aren't you?"

The distant howl of something that might have been a wolf—or a Death Dog—made them all look up suddenly. They huddled closer together on the log, closer to the fire, feeling the darkness grow deeper around them.

They set out again the next day, stopping more often to rest for the baby's sake. They halted by the edge of a wide road to eat their midday meal. Willow felt his spirits rise, knowing that they were in Daikini lands now and soon their journey would end. As he patiently changed the baby's rag diaper, the sound of hoofbeats echoed down the road. Catching her up, Willow scrambled down the embankment into the bushes with the others.

A band of Nockmaar soldiers thundered toward them, with two slavering Death Dogs running beside them. The soldiers halted almost in front of Willow's hiding place. A solitary rider, a Nockmaar officer judging from his uniform, rode toward them from the other direction. He reined in his horse and spoke with one of the soldiers while the rest of the troop rode on.

"The Nelwyns have the baby," the soldier reported. "We searched their village. A group of them are on the road somewhere."

"Find them!" the lieutenant ordered. "Widen the search and report to Sorsha!" They lashed their horses and galloped on. The Nelwyn band huddled in terror among the bushes.

"Let's go back!" Willow cried, clutching the baby tightly.

Meegosh nodded. "We'll take the baby with us."

"And lead those soldiers back there?" Vohnkar demanded. "They'll destroy our village. Our orders are to go to the crossroads. Come! We'll keep to the woods." Gathering up their supplies, they headed off into the underbrush.

Another exhausting day of hiding and struggling on through strange lands went by. At last Vohnkar stopped and pointed. "That's it. The crossroads." They went on, more cautiously than before. The Daikini crossroads was not a place with a good reputation.

Vohnkar and his men moved out into the open first, looking around them at scattered wagon parts, odd rubbish . . . and at the scaffold that dominated the meeting point. Flies buzzed in the silence around the two cages that hung from the scaffold, cages large enough to hold a Daikini. They were both occupied—or had been. All that was visible in one was a heap of rags. The other held a half-clothed skeleton;

one bony arm hung from the cage, forever pointing down.

Vohnkar didn't bother to investigate either cage more closely. "It's all right," he called. "Come on."

Willow and Meegosh emerged slowly from the bushes, staring at the grim spectacle with wide eyes. Willow glanced away along the deserted road and back again, shivering with more than the cold. "Where's Burglekutt?" he asked. They all turned, searching—and found their leader still cowering in the bushes behind them. Suddenly Willow felt better.

The Nelwyns made camp below the scaffold, glad when darkness finally hid the stark reminders of Daikini cruelty from their eyes. Willow set up a makeshift crib for the baby, trying not to hear too much in the eerie sounds of the night. "It's going to be all right, little bobbin," he said softly.

A hoarse snarl filled the darkness. Willow leaped to his feet in terror and stumbled back under one of the death-filled cages.

A hand reached down out of the night and yanked him off the ground. Willow screamed. The baby began to wail. The other Nelwyns stood frozen, gaping in amazement as a haggard Daikini slowly emerged from the pile of rags in the cage above their heads. He glowered down at them, his unshaven face looking like a demon's in the ruddy light of the fire. He held Willow suspended in midair. "Get me water, Peck, or di-i-ie. . . ." he hissed.

"I will. . . . Water. . . . Anything you say," Willow gasped.

The prisoner dropped him. Willow scrambled to the baby, picked her up, and rushed to safety behind Vohnkar and his warriors. Their spears shone in the firelight, pointing at the cage.

"You weaselly little Pecks!" the prisoner snarled. "Gimme water." He thrashed furiously inside the cage, hitting his head on the bars as he reached through them. He collapsed again, silent and exhausted.

"That's a Daikini," Burglekutt blurted. "We're in luck."

Willow held the baby closer. "We can't give her to him," he said indignantly.

"Somebody put him in there for a good reason," Meegosh pointed out.

Burglekutt grunted impatiently. "Ufgood, we've got to get rid of her. Those soldiers are after us—"

"Shh," Meegosh whispered, "he's looking right at us." They broke off talking and looked toward the cage again. The prisoner wiped a filthy hand across his filthy face and grinned encouragingly.

"We have to give the baby to somebody," Vohnkar said, wavering.

"I'm somebody," the prisoner rasped. "Lemme out and I'll take care of your baby." He pursed his cracked lips and made kissing sounds. The baby looked toward the sound and smiled. "See that? She likes me."

The Nelwyns gathered in a huddle, turning their backs on him. "I trust him completely," Burglekutt declared.

"But he tried to strangle me!" Willow protested.

"I wanna go home!" Burglekutt whined, looking and sounding less like a leader all the time.

Meegosh pointed down the road. "More Daikinis!"

The Nelwyns looked up hopefully as torches flickered in the distance. A horse-drawn wagon was ca-

26

reening down the road toward them. As it neared they heard voices—loud, drunken voices. They dove back into the bushes as the wagon thundered up to the crossroads.

Four wildly yelling, tattooed Pohas hung out of the wagon. Waving their torches, they set the cage that held the skeleton on fire. Then they turned and jabbed their torches into the other cage.

"No!" the prisoner yelled. "Help! Stop!" The cage burst into flames. The Pohas drove on, howling with laughter. He beat frantically at the blazing wood with his bare hands; his sleeves caught fire. "Thanks for your help, Pecks!" he screamed at the Nelwyns.

Willow and his companions scrambled out of hiding and began to throw dirt on the flames—and on the prisoner—until the fire was out.

"Are you all right?" Meegosh asked, looking up at him with concern.

"Me?" the prisoner said sourly. "Never better. They set me on fire!" He spat out a mouthful of dirt. "You wanna give your baby to them? They eat babies." He jerked his head at the retreating Pohas, rubbing his sore, burned arms.

"That's it," Burglekutt said. "We've got to get out of here. We're giving him the baby."

The prisoner nodded. "Good decision."

"No, Burglekutt!" Willow said. "We should wait."

Burglekutt stiffened. "Are you challenging my authority?"

Willow spoke up. "As far as this baby's concerned—yes."

"Don't listen to him, Burglekutt," the prisoner called.

Burglekutt flapped his arms in exasperation. "Fine,"

he said to Willow. "You stay here alone. But we're going."

"Wait—" the prisoner protested. "Not good . . . bad idea."

"Vohnkar?" Willow asked, turning to him for support.

"It's not his decision," Burglekutt snapped. He started to walk away.

"Burglekutt, you're troll dung!" Willow shouted.

"Willow!" Meegosh exclaimed. He had never heard his friend call anyone that. This was the village prefect! . . .

"Don't let him talk to you like that, Burglekutt," the prisoner urged.

Willow turned on him, furious. "You stay out of this!"

"Lemme outta here; I'll convince him." The prisoner shook his fist at Willow.

Burglekutt turned back to Willow, his own anger boiling over. "Listen, runt," he snarled, "while you're wasting your time here, your fields aren't getting planted. Think about it."

Willow didn't have to think for long, since he knew what was going through Burglekutt's mind. "Burglekutt, I'm gonna . . ." he began.

Burglekutt puffed out his chest. "You're gonna what?" He laughed, and Willow's nerve broke.

"Someday, Burglekutt, someday. . . ." he muttered.

"Vohnkar, let's go!" Burglekutt ordered.

Vohnkar looked back at the two friends as they started away. "Meegosh, are you coming?"

Meegosh bit his lip, looking at them and back at his friend. "I'm staying," he said.

Burglekutt's scornful laughter rang in their ears as

28

he trudged off with Vohnkar and the warriors.

"Burglekutt! Boys!" the prisoner shouted after them. "Don't leave me with these two. Let me out! At least gimme a drink of water!" he pleaded.

No one answered him except the wind howling through the trees. Willow rocked the baby gently, staring away down the road.

"What do we do now, Willow?" Meegosh asked in a small voice.

Willow shook his head. "I don't know."

"That was pretty stupid, Peck," the prisoner said scornfully.

"Don't call me a Peck." Willow glared at him. It was what Daikinis called Nelwyns, and it was not a flattering term.

"Peck!" the prisoner sneered. "Peck-Peck? Peck."

Willow reached into his pocket and pulled out the magic acorns. "You be careful." He held them up. "I'm a powerful sorcerer. I'll throw this acorn at you and turn you to stone!"

"You scare me to death, Peck." The prisoner made a face. "Go ahead. What are you waiting for?"

Willow looked down at the acorns and put them back in his pocket. The High Aldwin had warned him about using his magic in anger. A half-starved Daikini yelling insults from a locked cage was hardly a dire threat. "I wouldn't want to waste it," he muttered, embarrassed.

The prisoner laughed and shook his cage. "Peck!" he crowed. "Peck! Peck-Peck-Peck-Peck!"

Willow and Meegosh retreated into the darkness. The prisoner's mocking voice sang them to sleep.

Five

The sound of hoofbeats woke them in the morning. They sat up, blinking sleep out of their eyes as a messenger on horseback galloped by.

"What was that?" Meegosh mumbled, getting to his feet.

"Morning, boys," the prisoner called hoarsely with ingratiating good cheer. "Rough night, wasn't it?" His own rough night seemed to have convinced him that he would catch more flies with honey than with vinegar. "Did I introduce myself? Madmartigan." He stuck out a filthy hand.

Meegosh started forward, holding out his own hand uncertainly. "I'm Meegosh."

"Don't touch him, Meegosh," Willow warned, thinking that Meegosh had always been too naive for his own good. "He's dangerous." He glanced away as another rider came galloping toward them. "Stop!" he called, running out into the road. "Wait!"

The messenger shouted a warning and charged past without slowing down. Willow leaped aside, barely in time to avoid being trampled.

"He sure was breathing fire," Meegosh said, watching the rider's trail of dust.

Willow brushed himself off. "What's going on?" he asked.

"Smells like a battle," Madmartigan said.

"I suppose you're a warrior." Willow put his hands on his hips and gazed up at the ragged scarecrow swaying over his head.

"The greatest swordsman that ever lived," answered Madmartigan. He straightened up as much as the cage would allow and sliced the air with an imaginary sword. The motions were exotic and strange looking, but not all that convincing to Willow. Madmartigan settled down again and looked at them with tired eyes. "How about a drink?"

Meegosh was still staring up at him. "Gee, Willow, maybe he could help us."

Willow turned away. "Don't even listen to him," he said irritably. He went back to tend the baby, who was awake now and fussing. Then he picked up their water skin and poured himself a drink.

Madmartigan watched Willow and licked his parched lips. "These are bad times, my friend," he said to Meegosh. "Good men in cages, criminals running free. It doesn't pay to be honest. You a woodcutter?"

"Miner," Meegosh answered. "And my friend's a farmer."

"I knew it!" Madmartigan croaked. "Miners, farmers; you're victims! Yep, you and me, victims of a rotten, corrupt world. . . ." He pressed his forehead against the bars and began to make a sound that at first Willow couldn't identify. Then, with a shock, Willow realized that the prisoner was crying. Willow stared at him for a long moment. Was Madmartigan really crying or just trying to play a trick on them? At last he reached for the skin and poured out a cup of water. He took it to the cage. Even if the tears weren't real, the Daikini's thirst was. He could not watch someone die right before his eyes, even a Daikini rogue.

Madmartigan raised his head. "Thank you, friend," he said, with no trace of mockery in his voice. He put out his hand.

Willow turned away suddenly as another, totally unidentifiable sound reached him from the distance. "What's that?" he said.

Madmartigan grabbed at the cup of water held just out of his reach. "You hear trouble," he muttered.

"What is it?" Meegosh asked. The sound was becoming a deep rumbling now; the horizon swirled with dust.

Madmartigan swiped at the cup, missed it, and swiped at it again with exasperated persistence. "A hundred horses," he rasped, "five or six wagons . . . and about a thousand fools." He caught the cup at last as Willow turned back to look at him. He pulled it into the cage and gulped the water down.

Willow looked away again and saw an army slowly take form out of the swirling dust. Two cavalry officers appeared first, galloping toward him, followed by horsemen, foot soldiers, and wagons of supplies. Shields, swords, spears, and banners filled his field of vision with light and color to match the noise.

The two officers bellowed orders over the thunderous clamor of hoofbeats, marching boots, and clanking armor. Charging back and forth, they shepherded the army through the crossroads. Meegosh stood aside nervously as Willow pushed out into the melee, holding up the baby as he tried to attract an officer's attention. "Sir?" he shouted. "Sir!"

"Out of the way, Peck!" the officer barked as his skittish horse almost stepped on Willow.

Willow dodged back to Meegosh's side, still searching the throng for someone who might listen. Suddenly a large, bearded man rode up to the two officers. His armor was covered with dust, but his manner told Willow that this must be the commander of the troops. "We're close now," he shouted. "Attack at midday!"

The two officers split up, shouting orders as they charged away toward the front and rear of the column. The commander sat on his horse, watching as the army passed.

Gathering his courage, Willow scrambled forward again through the dust and confusion to the officer's side. "Sir! Sir!" he called. "We found one of your babies in our village. Will you take her?"

The commander looked down in surprise at the two Nelwyns and the baby. The sheer size of the Daikini, sitting astride an even larger horse, took Willow's breath away. "We're going into battle, little ones," the commander said, not unkindly. "Find a woman to take care of it."

"They thought you were a woman, Airk!" jeered Madmartigan from his cage.

The commander's head snapped around at the sound of the familiar voice. He stared, then frowned. "Well, I'll be. . . . Madmartigan," he said. "I knew you'd end up in a crow's cage."

"At least I'm not herding sheep." Madmartigan jerked his head at the passing troops. "What are you doing this far north?"

Airk Thaughbaer urged his restless horse forward until he sat eye to eye with the man in the cage. "The Nockmaar army destroyed Galladoorn," he said grimly.

"The castle?" Madmartigan asked, sounding incredulous.

Airk nodded. "It was a massacre. Bavmorda's on a rampage. Her troops are crushing everything in their way. We're going to try to stop them at the river Troon."

A spark showed in Madmartigan's eye. "Lemme out, Airk. Gimme a sword and I'll win this war for you."

Airk's face twisted with disgust. "After that stunt at Land's End you're lucky I don't kill you." His voice was as hard and cold as stone. He gave the cage a shove that set it swinging and turned his mount away.

"Airk!" Madmartigan cried.

Airk paused and looked back. "Madmartigan, I still serve Galladoorn. You serve no one, remember? Stay in your coffin and rot!" He rode on.

"I'll be around long after you're dead!" Madmartigan yelled with desperate fury. "You slime! I'm gonna cut your head off and stick it on a pig pole!"

"Friend of yours?" Willow asked mildly, looking up at him.

Madmartigan gave a snarl of rage. But then he took a deep breath. The anger disappeared from his face; his clenched fist loosened. He waved, wiggling his fingers, and grinned. "Hello . . ."

Willow stared at him, confused. Then he realized that Madmartigan was looking at the baby. The baby cooed softly, smiling back at him, as the army marched on by.

The army was long gone, but the two young Nelwyns were still at the crossroads and still no closer to finding help. Willow listened for the sound of more travelers but heard only the lonely wailing of the wind. He sighed, rocking the baby. "I miss Kiaya and the bobbins," he said.

Meegosh looked up from tending the fire. "Willow, we're running out of food. I'm getting scared," he said.

"Nobody's gonna look after your baby," Madmartigan called. He sat with his feet and arms hanging through the bars of his cage, staring at the Nelwyns. He had been staring at them that way for hours. "Know why? Nobody cares . . . except me. You wanna go back to your families. I could take care of that baby. I'll look after her like she was my own."

"I believe he would, Willow," Meegosh said tentatively.

Willow frowned, trying not to hear the same thing—he almost imagined it sounded like sincerity—in Madmartigan's voice. He would not weaken. He would not give a helpless infant to a lying Daikini just because he himself wanted to go home to his family. What if this were Mims or Ranon depending on strangers to take care of them? He glanced at Madmartigan. "He doesn't know anything about babies," he said sullenly.

"Ah, but I know a lot of women who do," insisted Madmartigan. He looked at the baby. "Why, if I had somebody, a little daughter, for instance, I'd have a reason to go on living." He looked up again, and

Willow saw the fleeting, almost thoughtful expression vanish from his face. He grinned, swinging an arm, and began to whistle hoarsely as if he had all the time in the world, and they didn't.

"He's a warrior, Willow," Meegosh ventured.

"You can't let me die here when all I want to do is protect her!" Madmartigan held out his hands to them with an earnest, slightly desperate smile.

Willow touched Kiaya's braid, biting his lip, and looked at the baby, then back at Madmartigan. At last he nodded reluctantly. Meegosh rushed over with an ax and hacked open the chain on the cage, dumping Madmartigan out onto the ground.

Willow stepped forward, carrying the baby. "You gotta promise to feed her," he said, his throat tight.

Madmartigan got to his knees, brushing himself off. Willow half expected him simply to leap up and run off, and half wished he would. But Madmartigan grinned and held his arms out to the baby with surprising good cheer. "Come to daddy, little darlin' . . ."

"And keep her clean," Willow ordered.

"Absolutely." Madmartigan took the baby carefully. "You like Madmartigan, don't you?" Still kneeling, he tickled her under the chin and winked at her as he fastened Willow's pack on his back. The baby gurgled and cooed.

Willow watched, frowning, half with worry and half with jealousy. "Here are her diapers." He handed over the rags. "Here's her milk bladder."

"Any milk in there?" Madmartigan asked.

"It's for her," Willow snapped.

Madmartigan looked at him. "I wouldn't steal milk from a baby," he said, annoyed. "You worry too

36

much, Peck."

"Willow," Meegosh corrected.

"I mean, Willow," Madmartigan repeated, without sarcasm this time. "You've done the right thing."

Willow took the baby from Madmartigan, held her one last time, and kissed her. "Bye," he said softly. He settled her into the pack on Madmartigan's back.

Madmartigan climbed to his feet a little unsteadily and shrugged the pack into a more comfortable position. Then he gave them a jaunty salute. "Good-bye, boys!" He swung around and started off down the road.

"Please take good care of her!" Willow shouted after him.

Madmartigan looked back. "I give you my word of honor!" He waved.

Meegosh sighed with relief and began to smile. But Willow frowned until Madmartigan was out of sight, still not convinced that his choice had been the right one.

Meegosh pulled at his arm, tugging him around. Before Willow could bring himself to take a step, Meegosh was half a mile down the road in the other direction. "Meegosh!" Willow cried, running after him. "Slow down!"

"Come on!" Meegosh called. "If we hurry we'll be home by tomorrow morning. I can't wait to see the expression on everybody's faces. We'll be heroes!"

"You really think so?" Willow panted, catching up with him.

"Sure." Meegosh nodded. " 'Look, it's Willow and Meegosh! The heroes have come home!' "

" 'Welcome back, boys!' " Willow chimed in, getting into the spirit of it. " 'You deserve medals!' "

" 'Let's make Willow Apprentice Aldwin.' "

" 'Or better still, High Aldwin!' " Willow laughed, then broke off suddenly. "Did we do the right thing, Meegosh?"

"Absolutely!" Meegosh nodded. "There's nothing to worry about."

A cry sounded in the distance. They spun around and saw an enormous eagle flying toward them over the trees. A tiny brownie warrior rode on its back, and clutched in its claws was the baby, still in her pack. The eagle dove low over their heads, sending them sprawling in the dirt.

Willow scrambled to his feet as the eagle flew on into the forest. Shouting and waving his arms, he ran after it. "Hey! Stop! Bring her back!"

"Willow!" Meegosh shouted, but Willow never heard him.

Willow ran on into the trees, desperately trying to keep the eagle in sight, never noticing how narrow the path ahead of him grew.

Tiny arrows rained down on him, stinging him like bees as he ran. More brownies were attacking him from hiding places in the trees. He plucked the arrows out as he raced on, only slowing as he reached a sudden fork in the road. He chose a path at random and started down it; then he saw ropes and nets waiting for him. He ran back to the fork. Meegosh was waiting for him there. "That way's a trap!" Willow said, pointing.

Together they started down the clear path—

"Oh noooooo!"

—and plunged into a pit hidden under leaves and branches. And that was the last they remembered.

Six

Willow woke as the contents of a very small pail of water splashed into his eyes. He tried to move and found that his wrists and ankles had been securely bound. Several brownies stood around him, pointing and laughing. The tiny wild men of the fairy forest wore loincloths, beaded necklaces, and sandals; their hair stood on end and their faces were painted lurid colors. They had done everything they could to make themselves look frightening to their enemies. Considering that none of them was more than ten inches tall, they needed all the help they could get, Willow thought. But then, he was the one who was tied up, and their prisoner. . . .

He looked around in the light of a dozen tiny bonfires. Meegosh moaned in pain somewhere near him. "Where am I?" Willow mumbled, blinking again. "Meegosh, are you all right?"

"I think my arm's broken." Meegosh groaned.

The brownie who had ridden the eagle strode forward to stand by Willow's face. "I am Franjean, king of the world!" he announced. The other brownies snickered, spoiling the effect. A few fragile, glowing fairies, as lovely as spring flowers and even smaller than the brownies, fluttered around Willow's face, tickling him.

"Where's that baby?" Willow demanded. "She's my responsibility!"

Franjean smacked Willow's nose with the back of his hand. "Keep quiet, you fool."

"Do that again and I'll kill you, you little . . ." Willow muttered.

"I'm not afraid of you Nelwyns," Franjean said. "You think you're so big." He smacked Willow again.

"Franjean!" A strange, melodious voice echoed above them. "Bring the Nelwyn to me."

Another brownie shuffled up to Franjean. "Uh-oh," he said. "Cherlindrea!" The other brownies began to gather around, taking hold of the ropes that bound Willow and Meegosh. "You're in trouble now," he said to Willow.

"No talking to the prisoner, Rool!" Franjean ordered.

"Well, *you* did," Rool protested.

"That's different," Franjean said. "I'm in charge." Willow struggled angrily, and Franjean leaped up onto his chest, waving a staff made of twigs.

"Hey, what's going on?" Willow demanded.

"Shut up or I'll break your nose," Franjean snarled. "You're mine to toy with! Forward!"

"Ouch! Get off me!" Willow shouted, without effect. The brownies hauled him and Meegosh away.

As the brownies dragged them deeper into the enchanted forest, the night around them was filled with a luminous galaxy of fluttering fairies. But Willow was in no position to enjoy the sight. Franjean poked and whacked him with his staff.

"When I get loose I'm gonna mash you!" Willow said, furious.

Franjean laughed madly, waving his staff. "You'll never break these bonds, loppy ears."

"Release the Nelwyn!" The mysterious voice that had ordered them deeper into the woods rang through the air again.

Willow smiled malevolently as a look of terror suddenly crossed the brownie's face.

"Uh-oh," Franjean muttered. The other brownies obediently cut the ropes. Willow jumped to his feet, towering over them, and they scattered into the underbrush like squirrels. He turned back when a strange glow began to pulse behind the trees.

"Welcome to my kingdom," the voice said, seeming to come from everywhere at once. Radiant beams of light pierced the forest around him, illuminating a cradle and the lost baby peacefully asleep inside it. Willow ran to her side as a beautiful woman materialized inside the blinding light. "I can't see anything," Willow murmured. The glow had become so intense that he couldn't make out the woman's form.

"I'm sorry . . ." the voice said. The light faded until Willow could see her clearly. She was beautiful, with long, flowing hair and luminous eyes. He realized that this must be Cherlindrea, who ruled over the legendary fairy forest with her magic. "Honey of nightingale for our honored guest," she called softly. "I'm so glad to meet you, Willow Ufgood."

The brownies emerged from hiding and began to bustle around, bringing Willow refreshments. Willow accepted a drink in a cup-shaped leaf, watching Franjean and Rool collide in their haste to serve him.

He smiled as both of them landed on the ground. Fairies twinkled about his face like fireflies, giggling. "How did you know my name?" he asked Cherlindrea.

Cherlindrea disappeared suddenly and reappeared next to the baby. "Elora Danan told me. Elora, Willow's here," she said to the baby.

The baby opened her eyes and looked up at them.

"She's just a baby," Willow said, unable to believe that she could possibly know such things.

"Elora is very special," Cherlindrea explained. "She is the daughter of the sun and moon . . . the future empress of all kingdoms."

Willow smiled. "That's a relief. Now I can go home."

"No, Willow." Cherlindrea raised her head. "Your journey has just begun."

"You don't understand," Willow protested. "I've got to go back to my family. I'm worried. They need me."

Cherlindrea shook her shining head. "It is you who don't understand, Willow. Elora Danan has chosen you to be her guardian." She lifted her hands, and the baby drifted up out of the cradle, floating in the magic cloud of light.

"Me?" Willow asked in disbelief.

"Yes." Cherlindrea nodded. "She likes you."

Willow caught the baby out of the air, afraid she might fall. Cherlindrea flickered out of sight and reappeared again. She held a wand in her hand now. It looked like a simple twig, but as she held it out to him, Willow could feel the power radiating from it.

"Here," Cherlindrea said, "take my wand to the sorceress Fin Raziel. She will help you take Elora Danan to the kingdom of Tir Asleen, where a good king will look after her."

"Why can't you do it?" Willow said. "You've got magical powers."

Cherlindrea shook her head again, sadly. "I wish I could, but my presence cannot extend beyond these woods."

"You need a warrior for a job like this," Willow objected. "I'm a nobody." He looked down at the baby. "You don't want me, Elora." Looking up at Cherlindrea again, he said, "Tell her. I'm short. Even for a Nelwyn!" He heard indignant grunts and glanced down at the brownies frowning up at him from around his feet.

The glow in the air intensified, so that Willow backed away, clutching the baby tightly. "Elora Danan must survive," Cherlindrea said, her voice ringing. "She must bring about the downfall of Queen Bavmorda, whose powers are growing like an evil plague." Cherlindrea swirled around him like a golden wind. Then, suddenly, there was silence and total darkness.

Willow stood alone in the dim moonlight, holding the baby. "Hello?" he called, his voice trembling.

Cherlindrea's voice echoed out of the darkness. "All creatures of good heart need your help, Willow. Soon Bavmorda will control the lives of your village, your children . . . everyone." One by one the fairies winked on again, flickering among the branches over- head. Cherlindrea reappeared out of the darkness, a great, shining presence among the trees. Again she offered him the wand. The brownies crept out of hid- ing. Willow felt all their eyes on him. "I cannot make you go, Willow," Cherlindrea said. "The choice is yours."

Seven

The dawn of a new day crept silently into the forest. The brownie fires had burned low when Rool tiptoed through the trees, carrying a sack of glittering dust. He sprinkled some of the dust onto the lovely eyes of a sleeping fairy, just as Franjean came up behind him.

"Where'd you steal that Dust of Broken Heart?" Franjean demanded.

"Nowhere." Rool shrugged guiltily. "I was just having fun."

"It belongs to the fairies!" Franjean snapped. "It's dangerous. Give that to me." He tugged at the sack, sent Rool tumbling, and hooked it onto his own belt. The sleeping fairy stirred at the noise and sat up, rubbing her eyes. Seeing Franjean standing in front of her, she gave him a lovelorn grin, leaped up, and smothered him in a barrage of kisses.

"Get away! Help!" Franjean bellowed. "Throw water on her!"

Willow stepped past the thrashing brownies to Meegosh's side and whispered, "Wake up, Meegosh.

It's time to go home."

"Home?" Meegosh mumbled. He scrambled up with a sudden smile.

"How's your arm?" Willow asked. "Think you'll be able to make it?"

"Oh yeah, it's fine!" Meegosh exclaimed. "Perfect! They put something on it." But he couldn't help rubbing it just the same, and Willow knew that he wasn't telling the whole truth.

"Listen," Willow said slowly. "I want you to tell Kiaya I love her and I think about her every day. . . ."

"Willow—" Meegosh's smile faded.

". . . and tell her I'm not going to let anything happen to the baby."

"You've made up your mind?" Meegosh asked, staring at his friend. Willow nodded. "It's gonna be dangerous, Willow—maybe I should go with you."

Willow shook his head. "Not with that arm, Meegosh. Give Mims and Ranon a hug for me. And don't let Kiaya worry."

"You sure you know what you're doing?" Meegosh said, frowning with concern.

Willow shrugged. "I hope so."

"Be careful." Meegosh put a hand on his friend's arm. "Daikinis say one thing and mean another." The two Nelwyns hugged each other in farewell, and Willow went on his way.

Willow soon discovered that he had inherited the brownies Franjean and Rool as his guides. It was not an entirely happy arrangement, but it was better than wandering through the forest and the world beyond it completely alone.

"This way! This way!" Franjean shouted with his usual insufferable arrogance.

Carrying the baby, Willow followed as patiently as he could. "Will it take long to find this Raziel?"

Franjean shook his head. "Not long."

"She's been exiled to an island just over those hills," Rool said, and pointed.

"She's been what?" Willow stopped short.

"By the evil Queen Bavmorda!" finished Rool.

"Rool, you fool!" hissed Franjean. "He doesn't need to know everything!"

"What are you saying?" Willow demanded. "What do you mean, island?" He shook Cherlindrea's wand at the brownies, who ducked.

"Don't play with that," Franjean warned him. "Cherlindrea told you: it holds vast powers. Only a great sorcerer can use it—not a stupid Peck like you!"

A branch smacked Willow in the face, emphasizing the point. "Are you sure you know where you're going?" he said.

"Of course!" said Franjean. "With us as your guides no harm will befall you—"

"Death below!" Rool suddenly shrieked in terror, pointing down the hill. Willow ran toward the edge of the trees. In the valley below hundreds of Nockmaar soldiers and cavalry were fighting the ragtag squad of rebel troops Willow had seen at the crossroads. Even from here he could hear the clash of weapons and the cries of dying men. "Daikinis. . . ." he murmured.

The overpowered rebel troops were being forced up the hill toward their hiding place. Willow watched, hypnotized, until suddenly a sound made him spin around. Behind him was a troop of black-armored Nockmaar soldiers. He crouched in the bushes, frozen with fear, as the hideous face of the Nockmaar general Kael loomed above him. But Kael's attention was on the distant battle. "No mercy!" he roared. He lowered his ominous death mask over his face and spurred his horse down the hill, and the rest of the cavalry followed, closing the trap on the doomed rebels below.

Willow and the brownies stumbled and scrambled for their lives, dodging horse after horse as the Nockmaar reinforcements thundered by. Elora Danan wailed and cried as Willow ran with her back through the forest, following the brownies, while behind them the Nockmaar troops descended on the rebel squad and crushed them.

"Shhh, don't cry, Elora," Willow murmured, his own voice unsteady as he huddled with her in the safety of the forest. "Things can't get any worse than this. . . ."

Or could they? A few hours later, Willow was trudging along a muddy road through the rain, trying in vain to keep Elora Danan's head dry and feeling utterly miserable. Up ahead through the gray mist he could see a tavern, its open bottom story stabling several horses. A decrepit wagon sat in the yard while someone worked in the rain to repair it. Willow walked faster, heading toward the welcome shelter.

Rool poked his head out of Willow's pocket and Franjean peered from his perch under Elora Danan's pack as they felt Willow change direction. "We're not going in there," Franjean said.

"Elora needs fresh milk," Willow answered firmly. He ducked into the stable and dashed toward the stairs that led up to the inn.

"You're not in command here, shorty," Franjean barked. "I am! We're not going inside and that's an order! You hear me?"

Willow didn't answer as he climbed the stairs. A minstrel's music greeted his ears when he entered the tavern's main room and stopped to look around. The place was packed with Daikini travelers waiting out the rain: nomad families, mothers with babies, local drunkards, and what looked to Willow like cutthroats and thieves of all kinds mingled in wary coexistence. As he watched, two Pohas crashed down from a balcony, fighting tooth and nail.

Mustering his courage, Willow raised his voice and called, "Could you spare some milk for this poor hungry baby?"

"Get outta here, Peck!" someone shouted. People began to pitch things at him, yelling "Beat it, Peck!" "Stick him on a spit!" "Cook him!"

Willow ran to a stairwell and took cover. Franjean poked his head out from beneath the pack and lowered himself precariously toward Willow's pocket just as Rool began to climb out, his eye on a pretty barmaid. "Look at her!" he said. "Give me that Dust of Broken Heart, Franjean."

"No!" Franjean clutched the pouch. "You can't have it!"

Rool grabbed it away from him—and pitched backward out of the pocket. He landed beside a large striped cat and dust spilled into his eyes. Stunned, Rool rubbed his eyes. He blinked them open and grinned amorously at the cat. "You are so beautiful!" he murmured. He flung his arms around the cat and kissed it. The cat hissed and yowled, flailing at him

48

with its claws. Rool leaped back in terror and tumbled headfirst into a vat of beer.

Willow ignored him, having more important concerns on his mind. Elora Danan whimpered with hunger as he looked around the room. At last Willow spotted a pail of milk on the floor next to a nomad family. "I could use your help, Franjean," he said. He felt his pocket twitch and looked down; Franjean cowered inside it. Willow sighed and put his finger into Elora Danan's mouth for a pacifier, quieting her as he began to edge toward the milk.

"Willow?" Franjean's muffled voice called.

"Shhh, quiet," Willow muttered and slapped his pocket. Stretching out his arm, he dipped a cloth in the bucket of milk. Nearby an ugly little Daikini boy made a face at him. Frowning, Willow took the soaked cloth and hurried back under the stairs to feed Elora Danan.

The boy followed him. As Elora Danan sucked hungrily on the cloth, the boy suddenly poked his head around the stairs and glared at Willow. Willow leaped back against the wall with a startled cry. The bottom plank of the wall gave way; he fell through into the room beyond.

As Willow tumbled into the room, he saw two women getting dressed in a panic. "Hurry! Hurry!" the prettier of the two gasped. "He's coming!" She peered out the window.

The other woman wore a kerchief over her hair. Powder rose in clouds as she patted thick makeup onto her face. "How do I look?" she asked gruffly.

Willow froze at the sound. He'd know that voice anywhere. It was Madmartigan. "Not you!" he cried before he could stop himself.

Madmartigan spun around and stared at him. "Where the devil did you come from?"

"I knew I shouldn't have trusted you," Willow said angrily. Franjean peeked out of his pocket.

"You're crawling with brownies," Madmartigan observed.

The pretty woman shrieked, "I hate brownies!"

Just then the bedroom door slammed open, and someone stormed in. Someone big, half drunk, and mean looking. "Where is he?" he roared.

Madmartigan wrapped a muffler hastily around his throat while the woman curtsied to the stranger. "There's nobody here except me and my, um, cousin." She turned to Madmartigan. "Hilda, this is my husband, Llug."

"Hilda?" Willow said, louder than he needed to.

Llug shoved his wife aside and glared at Madmartigan. Madmartigan batted his heavily made-up eyes and giggled. "How do you do?"

Llug sniffed at him, smelling perfume, and ogled his well-padded chest. When he put out a hand to test its authenticity, Madmartigan ducked away and snatched the baby from Willow's arms.

"Hey!" Willow shouted. "Give her back!"

Madmartigan *tsk*ed and shook his head. "These Pecks make terrible nursemaids."

"Nursemaid?!" Willow said, even louder. He began to leap at Madmartigan, trying to reach Elora Danan.

"They get too excited." Madmartigan batted him aside with one large hand, hugging the baby to his chest.

From the corner of the room came a loud burp. "Excuse me," Rool said, dripping beer. "Are we having a party?" Willow scooped him up and stuffed him into a pocket, muffling Rool's hiccups.

Llug trailed Madmartigan around the room, finally cornering him by the door. "Wanna breeeeed?" he leered.

"No, thank you . . ." Madmartigan murmured. "Time to leave." He jerked open the door and ran out. He didn't get far. Willow watched as several Nockmaar soldiers met him head on and herded him back into the room.

The soldiers dragged Madmartigan, Willow, and Llug and his wife out to the main room. Other soldiers stormed through the tavern, grabbing babies from frightened mothers and inspecting them. The brownies squabbled loudly in Willow's pocket as a tall woman in armor strode up to them. It was Sorsha, Bavmorda's daughter. "You!" She pointed at Madmartigan. "Are you the mother of that child?"

Worried more about Llug standing beside him than anything else at the moment, Madmartigan nodded. "Yes, yes, of course."

"Let me see it," Sorsha ordered.

"No!" Willow cried. "Don't let her!"

Sorsha shoved him aside with her boot. "I gave you an order, woman." She grabbed at the baby. Madmartigan elbowed her away, knocking her off balance. The soldiers reached for their swords as her lieutenant pointed a dagger at Madmartigan's throat. Sorsha drove her own sword into the floor like a spike and pulled off her helmet. Her long, wild red hair tumbled down over her shoulders.

Stunned by her unexpected beauty, Madmartigan stared. "By glory . . . you're beautiful. . . ." he said, barely remembering to keep his voice high.

"You're very strong," Sorsha answered, with a

startled, then suspicious look.

"Thank you," Madmartigan whispered, glancing down.

Sorsha peered at him and frowned. Suddenly she ripped away his kerchief and muffler. "You're no woman," she snapped.

"Not a woman?" Llug snarled.

Madmartigan grinned guiltily. "Gentlemen? Meet Llug." He ducked, just as Llug lunged at him. The fist that had been meant for his own face connected with Sorsha's lieutenant instead.

Madmartigan dashed to the window with the baby under his arm. He knocked Sorsha aside and leaped out of it as Llug and the lieutenant crashed to the floor, grappling. Seizing the opportunity, the other tavern patrons stampeded in all directions, looking for a way out. Willow dove out the window, following Madmartigan, as a furious Sorsha ordered her soldiers after them.

Eight

Madmartigan grabbed hold of a dangling rope as he pitched out the second-story window. He swung down from the balcony into the decrepit wagon sitting in the yard below. Settling the baby beside him, he grabbed up the horse's reins and drove away.

"Madmartigan! Wait!" Willow shouted. He ran frantically along the tavern balcony and leaped, closing his eyes, as Madmartigan rattled past below. With brownies spilling from his pockets, he landed on the sacks in the back of the wagon. Madmartigan tore out of the yard as if the devil was on his tail, leaving soldiers in the mud and chaos behind him.

The wagon swerved and fishtailed down the muddy road. Franjean and Rool clung to each other desperately to keep from being tossed out. Willow huddled under the seat, bumping his head as he settled Elora Danan into a storage box packed with straw. "Stop!" he shouted at Madmartigan. "Slow down! Stop!"

But Madmartigan yelled and slapped the reins, since he saw three Nockmaar horsemen and a war chariot closing in on him. The panic-stricken cart horse galloped even faster, but two of the soldiers soon pulled even with him. One soldier leaped into the wagon; the other took aim at Madmartigan with his bow.

"Stop this wagon, Madmartigan!" Willow shouted again, not able to see what was going on up above. "You're going to get us killed!"

Madmartigan watched as the archer took aim at him. Letting go of the reins at the last second, Madmartigan pitched backward into the wagon bed. The arrow meant for him struck the Nockmaar minion behind him. Before Madmartigan could reach the reins, yet another Nockmaar soldier leaped from his horse into the wagon to attack. They struggled together as the jouncing, driverless wagon sped on.

Willow climbed out from under the seat and tried to reach the dangling reins. The wagon hit a tree root and bucked him forward into the harness. Willow clung there desperately, suspended above the flashing hooves and the road. With a strength he didn't know he had he held on, and inched his way slowly and painfully back onto the wagon seat.

Madmartigan finally managed to hurl the soldier he'd been fighting off the back of the wagon. Willow gasped with relief. But the chariot was still on their trail. Its driver held the reins between his clenched teeth as he raised his arm to hurl a deadly bolo blade.

Willow grabbed the reins and jerked hard on them, stopping the wagon short. The chariot shot on by, its driver caught off guard. Willow dove under the seat to see to the baby.

"What are you doing?" Madmartigan yelled. "Are you crazy?" The chariot did a U-turn in the road and started back for them.

"You can't chase around with Elora like this!" Willow shouted. "We're getting off!"

Madmartigan grabbed the reins from his hand and drove the horse forward again, tumbling Willow into the back of the wagon. Yelling wildly, he sent the wagon straight at the chariot.

"Madmartigan, I mean it—" Willow gasped furiously. "I don't want to have to hurt you!"

Madmartigan drove on, still on a collision course, as if there was no one else in the wagon or on the road ahead. At the last second the chariot driver's nerve broke, and he veered aside. Madmartigan whacked him with a spear as he hurtled by. The chariot toppled over and crashed into a tree.

Madmartigan pulled the lathered horse to a halt at last. "*Now* we stop, Peck," he panted.

Willow pulled the crying baby out from under the seat and jumped to the ground with her. The brownies hopped down behind him. "What a stupid Daikini," Franjean grumbled, shaking himself out.

"You never, *ever* drive that fast with an infant!" Willow shouted.

Madmartigan frowned, waving his hand. "I just saved that infant's life." He whacked the horse on its flank, sending the wagon on down the track. Then he turned, hustled Willow into the ditch at the roadside, and made him lie flat.

Franjean leaped after them when he heard the sound of hoofbeats. Up above, Rool still stood in a stupor on the road. "Where am I?" he groaned.

Sorsha and her troops thundered past, and Rool tumbled into the ditch beside them.

When the riders were gone, Willow raised his head. "I knew I shouldn't have trusted you." He looked at

Madmartigan, remembering the argument that they had begun before all this happened. "You swore on your word of honor you'd look after Elora Danan."

"I did!" Madmartigan said defensively. He climbed to his feet, not meeting Willow's eyes. "But I was attacked . . . by a huge, hairy, vicious, smelly . . . cyclops. . . ."

"I am not smelly!" Franjean shrieked.

Rool nodded tipsily. "Franjean stole the baby while you were taking a—"

"Get outta here!" Madmartigan stamped his foot, and the drunken brownie toppled over.

"You're no man of honor," Willow said bitterly.

Madmartigan looked back at him. "I was once the greatest knight in the kingdom of Galladoorn," he muttered. He picked up a stick and thrust and parried it like a sword, but his balance was off, and the stick went flying.

Willow watched him in disgust. "You're reckless," he said.

Franjean helped Rool to his feet. "And irresponsible," he added.

"And dangerous!" Rool gasped.

"I declare we execute him." Franjean raised his tiny sword.

"I don't need this." Madmartigan waved a hand at them all in disgust. "I'm on my way. I gotta find some people my own size." He glanced at the baby with a wry, fleeting smile. "Good-bye, skinny."

"She's not skinny," Willow snapped.

Madmartigan looked pained. "Look at her arms. They look like a couple of sticks. He's not feeding you enough, is he?" He tickled the baby, and she giggled. Then he blew her a kiss and started away. As he climbed the hillside, dogs howled in the distance. Madmartigan stopped, glancing back. "You better clear out, Willow, before those troops come back!" he called.

Holding the baby, Willow watched Madmartigan go on his way with a sudden sinking feeling. Rool hiccuped and fell on his face. "Stand up straight," Franjean hissed. "We are an army."

"We don't need him, Elora," Willow murmured, still watching the Daikini grow smaller in the distance. Elora Danan began to cry. Willow stood where he was a moment longer, undecided. Then, "Wait, Madmartigan!" he shouted, and began to run up the hill.

He struggled through the tall grass, making all the speed he could, with Rool and Franjean following behind.

Madmartigan kept walking without looking back. "Go home, Willow," he said wearily. "I thought you didn't trust me."

"I don't," Willow panted as he came up alongside. "But we need your help."

"My help?" Madmartigan grimaced. "A great sorcerer like you? What do you need my help for?"

"You're a warrior and a swordsman and you're ten times bigger than I am, stupid!" Willow shouted, exasperated.

Madmartigan glanced down at him. "Are you trying to make my life more difficult than it is?" he asked bleakly. In the distance dogs bayed again, and soldiers shouted. Madmartigan threw himself down in the weeds. Willow crouched down beside him. "Look," he said, "I'm sorry I got angry." Now that he had time to think about it, he realized that

Madmartigan's courage and skill really had saved them all. "We wouldn't have escaped without you."

Madmartigan looked back at him, then squinted at the baby. He scratched her head with a friendly hand, as if she were a puppy. But he only said, "Yeah, well, don't expect me to help you again," and looked away. When the sound of dogs and soldiers faded into the distance, they got to their feet and began to walk in silence.

"This way!" Rool staggered in a circle, pointing wildly at the sky.

"We go beyond that hill to the lake!" Franjean commanded, jerking Rool around.

"Aw, no—" Madmartigan struck his forehead in mock despair as he strode along beside Willow. "That's where *I'm* going!" Lengthening his stride as if he had made a decision, he swaggered past Willow to take the lead. "All right, all right. . . ." He nodded. "You can stick with me as far as the lake. But that's it. You're not going south, I hope."

"No," Willow answered, trying to disguise his relief. "Just as far as the lake."

"Good." Madmartigan glanced down at the brownies and waved his hands. "Mumbo! Jumbo! I'm hungry. Go find me some eggs or something. Now!"

The two tiny warriors scurried away, Franjean pausing only long enough to turn back and shout, "We are not afraid of you!"

Madmartigan grunted and turned back to Willow. "Ungrateful little creatures. . . ." They walked on.

Far away in Nockmaar Castle, Queen Bavmorda paced anxiously with her druids. She looked up as General Kael entered the echoing throne room, followed by two soldiers. "Kael," she snapped, "have you found the child?"

He bowed his head. "The search goes on, my queen."

She frowned, clenching her hands. "Why, with all my power, with the strength of my great army, can you not find this little child?" she demanded.

Kael hunched his shoulders. "We search even now," he muttered. "It won't be long."

Bavmorda's frown only deepened. "Find the child!" she shrieked. "Find the child! Time is running out!"

Kael backed away from her presence and hurried off.

Nine

The brownies slept restlessly beside the campfire. Madmartigan sat ripping apart his female clothes, reshaping them into something more suited to a fighting man. As he worked he watched Willow check Elora Danan, who lay sleeping. "She's kind of cute when she's asleep."

"She's really a princess, you know." Willow glanced up at him, wanting to explain why her safety was so important.

"And you're a great sorcerer, and I'm the King of Cashmere," said Madmartigan scornfully. "Go to sleep." He lay down and turned his back on them, shutting his eyes.

"Good night, Madmartigan." Willow sighed, still not sure what to make of his reluctant traveling companion or if they could really count on him. When he thought Madmartigan must be asleep, he pulled Cherlindrea's magic wand carefully from his pack. If only he could master this wand, his own magic could protect them. Unable to resist he shook it lightly, whispering "Tuatha . . . lawkathok . . . tuatha!"

Out of nowhere a bolt of lightning exploded around him, flinging him into the air.

Madmartigan sat up, shaking his head. "Willow?" he called. "Willow?" He looked up. Willow hung in the branches of a tree over his head. "Oh," he mumbled foggily, "there you are. Good night, Willow." He lay down and went back to sleep.

They traveled on the next morning, walking for a good part of the day without seeing anyone or anything that looked dangerous. At midday they stopped to eat below a roaring waterfall, the most splendid sight Willow had seen yet on his journey. He turned away from it reluctantly and saw Madmartigan holding the baby on his lap. The Daikini was letting her suck on a wild root. "What are you doing?" Willow demanded.

Madmartigan shrugged. "I found some black root. She loves it."

"Black root!" Willow cried, leaping up. "I am the father of two children. You never, ever give a baby black root!"

"My mother raised us on black root," Madmartigan said. "It puts hair on your chest. Right, Sticks?" He took a generous bite from the root, to prove that it was harmless.

"Her name is not Sticks," Willow said, not even sure himself why the sight of Madmartigan holding the baby upset him so. "She's Elora Danan, the future empress of all kingdoms. And the last thing she's going to want is a hairy chest." He snatched the black root from Madmartigan's hand and flung it away.

They continued their journey in silence. At last

Franjean and Rool stopped on a hill overlooking a large lake. "There's the island!" Rool called.

"We made it!" Willow exclaimed, hardly believing his eyes.

"We'll get a boat in that village." Franjean pointed down the hill. Cautiously they began to descend the steep slope.

When they reached the outskirts of the village, they slowed, and their faces fell. Half a dozen decrepit huts sat rotting on the edge of the lake. The village had obviously been abandoned long ago. The travelers walked down its eerily silent street, silent themselves with grim disappointment.

All except Madmartigan. "Well, looks like I got you here," he said cheerfully, scrounging through the rubbish for anything that might still be valuable.

"You?" Franjean piped indignantly. "What did you do, you stupid Daikini? All you did was hang around and eat our eggs!"

"And eat and eat and eat!" Rool added.

Madmartigan frowned. "I'll eat you, you little—" He swiped at them.

Franjean leaped out of his way, clambering up the side of a ruined hut. "Daikini dog!" He spat.

"Yeah"—Rool echoed, peering out from behind a hut—"Daikini dog!"

Willow walked along the shore, ignoring the noisy argument as he searched for something they could use to get them to the island. At last he found a small boat that still looked sound, even after years of waiting for an owner who had never returned. "I found a boat!" he called. "We're all set." He laid Elora Danan down on the shore.

"Good," Madmartigan said, following the two

brownies down to the boat. "Take these two lizards out and drown 'em." He knelt by the baby. "Goodbye, Sticks," he said gently. He got to his feet and started to walk away.

"Madmartigan," Willow called.

Madmartigan spun around. "What!" he shouted.

"Thanks," Willow said.

Madmartigan shrugged, waved, and went on his way.

"I am going to miss him," Rool said sadly.

"Me too." Franjean nodded. "I enjoyed humiliating him."

Willow began to push the boat toward the lake.

"What are you doing?" a voice asked.

Willow looked up, startled. A golden-haired boy stood waist deep in the water in front of him. Franjean and Rool rushed to the baby's side, brandishing their spears. "I'm borrowing this boat to go out to that island," Willow said uncertainly to the boy.

"The island is cursed," the boy warned. "Don't go out there!"

"Cursed?" Willow repeated.

"Beware of the lake," the boy said. "Queen Bavmorda's powers control the elements here." He dove back under the water and disappeared.

"Cherlindrea said nothing about a curse," Rool murmured.

"I don't think we should go out there." Willow shook his head.

Franjean elbowed Rool aside. "That was just an odd boy. Pay him no mind. Fin Raziel is a most powerful sorceress. You *must* take the wand to her."

"She will save us," Rool agreed.

"I don't want to take Elora out there," Willow said.

"You're right!" Franjean nodded eagerly. "Leave her on shore."

"Oh yes!" Rool chimed. "We will stay here with her."

Willow looked out at the island again, frowning with worry. At last he sighed and nodded.

Willow carried Elora Danan to a hut and settled her inside it. "It's all right, Elora," he said. "Go to sleep. Nobody will find you here. I'll be back with Fin Raziel very soon."

The two brownies waved their spears. "We will guard her with our meager lives," Franjean said. They snapped to attention like soldiers. Willow kissed the baby and left the hut.

As he rowed the boat across the gray lake toward the island, he was more worried about leaving Elora Danan behind than about what he would find ahead of him. At last he reached the island and pulled his boat ashore near the shattered remains of a skeleton. "Raziel?" he called nervously. "Hello! Fin Raziel!" He walked forward under a large tree.

"What are you doing here?" a high-pitched voice demanded. "Get away!" Willow looked up. A furry creature looking something like a small possum scuttled down the tree to snarl viciously at him. "Go back!" it said. "Who are you?"

"I'm Willow Ufgood," Willow answered, hardly surprised at all to be having a conversation with a possum. "I'm here to find the great sorceress Fin Raziel."

"That's me!" the creature exclaimed. "I'm Raziel."

Willow shook his head. "This can't be right," he said.

"One of Bavmorda's spells transformed me," she snapped impatiently.

Willow shrugged, thinking that made as much sense as anything else. "Well, this wand is for you. It's from Cherlindrea." He held it out.

Raziel sprang onto his chest. "Cherlindrea!" she cried. "The prophecy was true, then. The princess has been born?"

"Yes," Willow said, "and she needs you."

A flock of birds rose from the tree, screeching, and flew off into the suddenly darkening sky. The wind began to rise, howling angrily.

"Hide the wand!" Raziel commanded. "Bavmorda knows of your presence here."

Willow gasped, turning back. "What about Elora Danan?"

"Hurry!" Raziel ordered. "Get in the boat! We must leave this island right now!"

Willow got them back into the water as quickly as he could. The waves tossed the small boat like a cork as the storm grew worse, and he clutched Raziel tightly against his chest to keep her safe. Suddenly she pointed a claw at the bow. He turned and saw a hand appear, and then a face. The golden-haired boy he had seen on the shore began to climb into the boat.

"Kill him!" Raziel cried.

"No!" Willow said, shocked.

"Kill him!" she insisted.

Willow hesitated a moment more, then grabbed up his oar and smashed the boy back into the lake. The boy surfaced again near the boat, leaping like a dolphin. His form began to change, becoming fishlike, as he dove and vanished again. He rose up once more—this time with monstrous jaws gaping. Willow bashed the fish beast with the oar and it pulled away again, with fishing nets trailing from its jaws. Too late Willow felt his feet jerk out from under him as the nets tangled around his ankles. He was dragged overboard and into the water.

Willow swirled along in the buffeting wake of the monster, struggling until he could cut himself free with his dagger. He kicked his way to the surface and swam frantically back toward the pitching boat. He heard a roar as the monster surfaced and lunged after him.

"Hurry, Willow!" Raziel cried. "Hurry!" Willow scrambled on board, gasping. The monster crunched wood behind him and drew back for another try. Willow dug into his pocket, pulling out a magic acorn . . . and dropped it. He fumbled desperately in the bottom of the leaking boat, found it again, and stood up—just as the monster's jaws opened, ready to swallow him down. He hurled the acorn into its gaping mouth.

The monster turned to stone before his eyes and sank beneath the waves.

Ten

Willow and Raziel barely made it to shore. Willow waded up the muddy bank at last and fell to his knees, coughing and spitting. He had to rest there a moment before he could get up and go to the hut where Elora Danan waited.

He showed Raziel the baby, lying peacefully asleep. "It *is* Elora Danan," Raziel murmured. "At last sky and earth rejoin. Isn't she beautiful. . . ."

"That's Raziel?" Rool whispered, staring at what appeared to be a talking possum.

Franjean shrugged. "I don't know," he muttered dubiously. "I expected something more grand . . . less fuzzy."

Raziel glanced at them, irritated. "Willow, you must use the wand," she said. "Turn me back into my human form."

Willow nodded. "Tell me what to do." He held the wand uncertainly, not even sure how to hold it.

"You're not a sorcerer?" Raziel asked, frowning.

"Yes—" Willow looked down suddenly. "Sort of," he mumbled. "Well, I'm a farmer. But I know a few tricks and . . ."

"Tricks?" Raziel cried, incredulous. "Cherlindrea sent *you*? You can't just learn sorcery—it takes years and years!" She ran around the hut, raging and squeaking.

Willow shrugged helplessly. "I'm sorry."

"Quiet!" she commanded, pulling herself together. "You must learn. Come away. There's an evil here!" She scurried out the door.

Willow picked up the baby and followed her.

He came out of the entrance and stopped dead. Madmartigan sat on a horse waiting for them . . . with three Nockmaar soldiers beside him. The two brownies ducked back inside, unnoticed, as Raziel tried to bolt away. One of the soldiers skewered her tail with his spear, stopping her escape.

"Hi, Peck," Madmartigan said with a guilty grin. "Sorry about this." He shrugged.

Willow glared up at him, speechless with anger. Why had he ever trusted Madmartigan? That worthless Daikini had betrayed them, he thought.

The Nockmaar sergeant snarled, "Keep your mouth shut!" He knocked Madmartigan off his horse with a sudden, brutal blow. Madmartigan sprawled on the ground. Then Willow saw that Madmartigan's hands were bound behind him, his clothes were torn, and his back bore fresh, bloody lash marks. "You see?" the sergeant said sourly. "I told you we'd find them anyway."

More troops galloped up to the hut. A soldier dismounted, came toward Willow, and tried to take the baby from his arms. Willow fought him, kicking and punching with all his strength. "No! Get away from her! You can't have her! Leave her alone!"

Sorsha rode up with more of her men as the soldier knocked Willow to the ground. He handed the baby to her. "This is the baby we're looking for," she said. "We must take it back to Nockmaar."

"Your mother can't overturn the prophecy," Raziel cried, dangling ignominiously from a spear. "She hasn't the power."

"Fin Raziel"—Sorsha studied her with a mocking smile—"did you think my mother would let you escape?" At her nod, the soldiers tossed Raziel into a sack and tied it tightly. Madmartigan staggered to his feet in front of her, jostling a soldier aside. Sorsha stared at his tattered clothes from her saddle. "Lose your skirt?" she asked, raising an eyebrow.

"I've still got what counts," Madmartigan said, matching her stare with his own.

"Not for long." She kicked him in the jaw, knocking him off balance. Then she turned her horse and rode away.

The Nockmaar troops bound Willow's hands. Taking the prisoners with them, they rode away after their leader.

Franjean and Rool came out of hiding as the soldiers disappeared and ran after them down the road. But their tiny legs were no match for the Nockmaar steeds, and soon they flopped down in the dust, exhausted.

"We'll never keep up with those horses," Rool gasped.

"Then we'll have to track them," Franjean said.

"You don't know how to do that," Rool protested morosely. "Besides, it would take forever. And even if we find them, they'll catch us, stick us in a cage, torture us, and finally devour us."

Franjean looked at him. "Are you suggesting we go home?"

Rool thought about it. "No." He shook his head. "This is more fun."

They got up again and trotted down the road.

Sorsha and a caravan of fifty Nockmaar troops traveled on toward the snow-covered mountains where Nockmaar Castle waited. Raziel rode captive in a small cage in the back of a wagon. Willow and Madmartigan struggled along in the choking dust behind her, chained to the wagon by their necks. Willow had to take three steps for every one that Madmartigan took just to keep up the pace.

"I'm worried about Elora," Willow said. "She doesn't sound good." He could hear the baby crying up ahead; she had been crying all afternoon.

"Hurry!" Raziel called. "Try the chant again."

Willow tried to put Elora Danan out of his mind and concentrate on the spells Raziel had been teaching him. "Tanna . . . looth . . . I can't remember the middle part."

"Locktwarr!" Raziel said impatiently. "That's the word that pleads for change!"

"Locktwarr," Willow repeated with fresh determination. "Locktwarr. . . ."

Sorsha rode up beside them, glowing with the confidence of command as she controlled her prancing stallion. She slowed its pace to match theirs.

"Sorsha, you remind me of your father," Raziel said.

Sorsha frowned. "Don't insult me. He was a weakling."

"He was a warrior," Raziel answered gravely,

"and a great king."

"He was a traitor, an enemy of Nockmaar."

"Your mother has poisoned you," Raziel said.

Somewhere up ahead the baby cried again. "Elora's cold and hungry," Willow dared to interrupt. "She knows me. Please let me take care of her."

"I don't need help from a Peck," Sorsha sneered. She glanced away and caught Madmartigan staring at her. "What are you looking at?"

"Your leg," he said. His expression changed. "I'd like to break it."

Sorsha laughed. "You may find that difficult, slave, while I'm up here and you're down there."

Madmartigan strained against his bonds. "Then come down here and take this chain off my neck!"

Sorsha smiled. "I'll take it off at your funeral." She spurred her horse on up the line of troops.

Madmartigan rubbed his sore jaw. "I hate that woman."

Late that day a large Nockmaar camp came into view. Willow lifted his drooping head to see their destination more clearly. He stumbled and fell as his foot struck a stone. He was dragged along in the snow, too exhausted to fight his way to his feet again. Madmartigan ducked down and picked him up, hoisting the Nelwyn onto his own shoulders.

Death Dogs howled and fires burned in the ominous dusk ahead. A hulking figure rode out to meet them, silhouetted by the firelight: Bavmorda's general, Kael.

"Aw, no . . . Kael. . . ." Madmartigan muttered. "That's all I need."

Sorsha galloped up to Kael with the baby under

her arm. She showed Elora Danan to him, and he howled like a beast in triumph. They rode on into the camp together.

"What are they going to do with her?" Willow cried. But no one answered him.

When they arrived in the camp, more soldiers threw them into a makeshift prison cell and then left them there alone. Madmartigan stood keeping a lookout as Willow knelt over a bowl, mixing snow and dirt into a blob of mud. Raziel, still in her cage, hung from the roof of a nearby lean-to among stacks of skins and shields. She watched Willow work.

"Hither waltha bairn deru, bordak bellanockt . . ." Willow chanted.

"That's magic?" Madmartigan said dubiously. "It smells terrible."

"That's the life spark," Willow explained. "It forms after—"

"Well, it stinks," Madmartigan growled. "This whole thing stinks."

"Ignore him, Willow," Raziel said. "He's a fool." Madmartigan glared at her. "Repeat the incantations," she instructed, unruffled.

Willow stirred the mixture with Cherlindrea's wand. "Earth, water, sky. What's next?"

"Fire," she said. "It must be burned to a fine ash."

"How are we going to get fire?" Willow asked, frustrated. The torches were all out of reach.

Calmly Madmartigan dug a flint out of his pocket and scratched it against the cell. Sparks showered down. He grinned. " 'Ignore him, Willow,' " he repeated, glancing at Raziel. " 'He's a fool.' " He broke off, shoving the flint back into his clothes as someone approached their prison. It was General Kael.

Kael stared at Madmartigan. "I know you."

"No . . ." Madmartigan shook his head earnestly. "I'd remember you."

"Madmartigan," Kael snarled.

"N-no." Madmartigan backed up a step, beginning to sweat. "Madmartigan's dead."

"Good!" Kael rumbled. "He stole my woman."

"He stole mine too," Madmartigan said indignantly. "I killed him. I'm a master swordsman. Lemme out of here, I'll win this war for you."

Kael lunged forward, grabbing Madmartigan by the throat. He yanked him up to the bars. "This war's already won!" He flung Madmartigan to the ground and stalked away.

Madmartigan picked himself up, slowly and painfully. "If only I had a sword. . . ." he muttered. He gestured, going through the empty motions of exotic swordplay that were becoming all too familiar to Willow.

Willow sighed. "If only you'd quit talking about it." He went back to his work, but stopped and looked up again as he heard the baby crying. "Elora is sick," he said worriedly. "They're not taking care of her."

"Willow, worrying won't help her," Raziel said. "Finish your work! You must make the wand your own and change me back tonight."

"Tonight?" Willow protested. "I'm not ready."

"You'd better be," she said.

They all turned at the sound of boots approaching again. Willow folded the ball of mud into a piece of cloth and stuffed it into his clothes.

Sorsha's lieutenant unlocked the cell door and grabbed Willow, jerking him forward. "Peck!" he snarled. "You're coming with me." He dragged Willow out, slamming the door in Madmartigan's face as he tried to follow.

Eleven

The lieutenant hauled Willow to Sorsha's tent and shoved him inside. Willow got up and shook himself out, just as Sorsha stepped from behind a curtain, still in uniform and holding the crying, coughing baby. "There's something wrong with this baby," she said. "Make it shut up." She thrust it into Willow's arms impatiently.

"She has a fever," Willow said, feeling how hot Elora Danan's tiny body was even through her wrappings. "This is bad."

Sorsha frowned. "Do something, Peck."

"She's wrapped up too tight; she can hardly breathe. . . ." Willow began to loosen the blankets around her.

"Do you think she's hungry?" Sorsha asked, irritable and anxious all at once. "I tried to feed her, but she just spat it out. I'm not a mother."

The baby quieted as Willow made her comfortable. "My son, Ranon, had this cough and he almost died," he said, his mind racing. "We need lots of steam. Here. . . ." He held the baby out to her.

"No—" Sorsha stepped back. "She'll start crying again."

"Hold her up, on your left shoulder," Willow instructed. "She likes that."

Sorsha took the baby reluctantly, following his advice. Elora Danan lay against her shoulder, resting quietly, while Willow hooked a pot of water over the fire. With his back to Sorsha he took the pouch of mud from his pocket and set it ablaze.

"Who's that horrible friend of yours?" Sorsha asked, patting the baby's back awkwardly.

"You mean Madmartigan?" Willow asked.

"Madmartigan, yes," Sorsha answered, contempt dripping from the words. "Who is he?"

Willow shrugged. "I don't know very much about him."

"He's very bold," Sorsha said.

"He says he's a master swordsman," Willow volunteered.

Sorsha laughed. "We'll see about that. . . ." she murmured.

The mud flared up and burned to ash. Startled, Willow dropped it. He turned, facing Sorsha so that she wouldn't notice. "Bring Elora here, near the steam. Somebody will have to stay up with her all night to make sure she keeps breathing."

He saw fear flicker across Sorsha's face, just as he had hoped. She crouched down and handed him the baby. "Don't let her die, Peck," she said. "My mother needs her alive." She turned away and went back into the sleeping area of her tent. Quickly Willow scooped up the ash and stuffed it into his pocket. Then he settled down at Elora Danan's side to watch over her through the night.

◆ ◆ ◆

Madmartigan woke with a start as Willow was thrown back into their cell at dawn. "What happened?" he asked.

"Elora was sick," Willow said. "But she's going to be all right now." He looked up at Raziel. "Raziel, I did it. I fired the potion."

"Good, we are ready." Raziel nodded. "You must transform me. Quick. Get me down."

Willow picked up a stick and poked it through the bars, trying to reach her. The stick wasn't long enough. "Madmartigan—help me," he called.

Madmartigan got to his feet wearily and poked at the cage with the stick, straining as far as his arm would reach, barely keeping his balance. Abruptly the cage crashed to the ground and shattered; Madmartigan lost his balance, banged his head on the bars, and fell down. Raziel scampered up to his face and nipped his ear disdainfully. "Ow-ow-ow-ow!" Madmartigan yelled. "Willow, why don't you help me instead of chattering with this muskrat?"

"Muskrat!" Raziel exclaimed. "When I change back into my former self and can use Cherlindrea's wand, I will open this cell, crush this army, and take Elora Danan to Tir Asleen, where she will be safe!" She nipped Willow's finger this time.

"Ow!" Willow cried. "What did you bite *me* for?"

"You must put three drops of your blood in the potion," she said matter-of-factly.

"Well, you could have warned me. . . ." Willow muttered.

"Now," Raziel instructed, "rub it on the wand and make it your own."

Willow touched the wand with his bleeding finger,

putting all his attention into the task. Madmartigan watched, silent for once.

"What is a sorcerer's greatest power?" Raziel asked.

"His will," Willow answered, remembering the things she had taught him on the long journey here.

"Use it," she said. "Remember everything I have taught you. For beginners there is some pain, but don't let anything break your concentration."

The silence stretched as Willow held up the wand. He began to chant softly.

"We have arrived!" a high, arrogant voice announced. "Hello, everybody!" Franjean hopped into the cell.

"You are saved!" Rool cried, following him in.

"*Shhh!*" three voices echoed at once.

Franjean and Rool looked up, insulted, as Willow began to chant again.

"What are you gonna look like, Raziel, if this works?" Madmartigan asked.

"Quiet!" Raziel hissed. "Don't interrupt."

"Sorry," Madmartigan said, chastened.

"Luatha . . ." Willow chanted, "danalora . . ."

Raziel looked at Madmartigan again. "I am young and more beautiful than you could ever imagine."

Madmartigan glanced at the possum, and a sudden flicker of interest showed in his eyes. "Concentrate, Willow," he urged.

Willow closed his eyes, channeling every bit of his will into his work. "Danalora . . . avalorium . . . greenan luatha, danu, danu, danalora luatha danu!"

"No, Willow!" Raziel gasped. "You're losing me!" Her voice began to squawk oddly. Her body contorted, and her fur began to change into something else—into black feathers. With a shimmer of magical force, she was transformed into a bird. Willow collapsed on the ground, rubbing his sore wrist, and dropped the smoking wand.

"Uh-oh," Franjean muttered. "The Nelwyn butchered that one."

"Nice try, Willow." Madmartigan leaned down to help him up, finally impressed by the unquestionable power he had seen Willow wield. "You all right?"

But Willow's only concern now was his failure. He looked up at the raven. "Now how are we going to get out?" He shook his head in frustration.

"Oh!" Franjean brightened. "You want out?"

"Easy," Rool added. "We can pick the lock!"

"I'm sorry, Raziel," Willow said, still gazing at her.

"My fault!" she croaked impatiently. "You weren't ready. Farmers—Cherlindrea sends me farmers!" She ruffled her shining black wings.

The two brownies scrambled up the cell bars and began to pry the lock open with Franjean's spear. Madmartigan leaned over, studying their technique. Franjean elbowed Rool aside. "No, no, like this!"

"Here," Madmartigan said, "let me try."

"Get back, you stupid fat Daikini!" Franjean snapped. He whacked Madmartigan across the nose with his hip pouch. Sparkling Dust of Broken Heart flew into Madmartigan's face, and he rubbed his eyes, sneezing. The lock clicked open as the brownies gave it one last jab. "There!" Franjean exclaimed. "You are free."

"Come on, Madmartigan," Willow called, heading for the open door. "Let's get Elora Danan out of here."

Madmartigan straightened up with a dazed look on his face. He bumped into the doorway as he followed Willow out.

"Wait!" Raziel cawed. "What about me?" She flapped her wings in exasperation and flew up into the sky above their heads.

Willow led the way through the still-dark camp to Sorsha's tent, carrying Franjean and Rool. Ducking aside to avoid the patrolling guards, he looked back, wondering what was making Madmartigan so slow. The Daikini was sauntering along as if he were out for a spring stroll and staring at the sky. "Madmartigan!" Willow whispered.

"Look at the sky, Willow," Madmartigan said softly. "The sun's coming up, but you can still see the stars. Isn't that beautiful?"

Willow stared at him, nonplussed. Franjean and Rool glanced guiltily at each other, remembering the fairy dust. "Are you all right?" Willow asked.

"Never better." Madmartigan nodded. "I feel . . . good." He smiled an easy, relaxed smile, as if the nearest enemy soldier were hundreds of miles away.

Willow shot him another dubious look and pulled up the back wall of Sorsha's tent. They peered inside. "I left Elora right there on those furs," Willow whispered.

"Only one of us should go in there," Madmartigan murmured. "I've had experience with this sort of thing. I know what I'm doing."

Right then Willow was not so sure about that, but he nodded.

"Hurry! Hurry!" Raziel cawed.

Madmartigan crawled inside. He stood up slowly, peering around in the dim candlelight until he spotted Elora Danan asleep in the far corner of the tent. He crept forward past Sorsha's bed. As he passed it

80

he looked down at her, then stopped. Out of her armor and wearing soft nightclothes, with her long red hair lying like satin around her, she looked like a sleeping goddess. He had never seen anyone so beautiful. He bent down and kissed her gently. As he pulled away again, he whispered, so softly that even he barely heard it, "I love you. . . ."

"Uh-oh," Rool muttered, as the others watched the scene unfold with horrified eyes.

"Madmartigan, what are you doing?!" Willow hissed. "Get going!" He waved his hand frantically.

Madmartigan glanced up, seeming to remember his duty again. But instead he pressed his hands to his heart and cried, "Oh, Sorsha! Awake from this hateful sleep! It deprives me of your beauty. The beauty of your eyes."

Sorsha's green eyes opened, blinked. And then a dagger flashed out from beneath her bed sheet, aimed at Madmartigan. "One move, jackass—" she snarled.

Madmartigan held out his hands to her. "You are my moon, my sun, my starlit sky. Without you I dwell in darkness. I love you!"

Willow gaped a moment longer, then crept into the tent, sneaking past the two unlikely lovers.

"What are you doing here?" Sorsha demanded, more incredulous than angry now.

"Your power has enchanted me and I stand helpless against it," Madmartigan said passionately. "Come to me now, tonight. Let me worship you in my arms."

"Get away from me!" Sorsha shouted, sure she was facing a madman now. Her dagger caught in his shirt and slit it right up to his throat. But the point stopped there, trembling.

"I love you," Madmartigan said.

"Stop saying that!" Sorsha cried.

"How can I stop the beating of my heart?" he asked. He caught her free hand and clasped it against his naked chest.

Her other hand pressed the dagger's point against his throat. "Out of fear," she snapped.

"Out of love," he insisted, with no fear at all in his eyes.

"I can stop it," she said fiercely. "I'll kill you."

"Death next to love is a trivial thing," declared Madmartigan. "Your touch is worth a hundred thousand deaths." He let go of her hand, but she did not pull it away from his chest. Instead her trembling body leaned toward him, as if it were drawn by some irresistible force, until their lips were close enough for a kiss.

And then suddenly the tent canvas tore open and Kael stepped inside, carrying Willow, who still clutched Elora Danan in his arms. "What's going on here?!" Kael bellowed. He hurled Willow and the baby onto a heap of straw as Sorsha pulled back from Madmartigan and saw the empty crib.

"Deceiver!" she cried. She lunged at Madmartigan again, raising her dagger. He rolled backward, kicking the dagger out of her hand and grabbing her sword, which lay beside her bed. Leaping up, he cut down the center pole of the tent. As the tent collapsed around them, he caught hold of her and finished what they had almost begun, giving her a passionate kiss.

The tent engulfed them all in darkness. Raziel flew in circles high overhead, screeching with distress as she looked down on the chaos below her. Bodies writhed under the fallen mass of canvas. And then a blade slit through the heavy cloth, flashing silver in the dawn light. Madmartigan leaped out, and as soldiers surrounded him he whipped Sorsha's sword around him in the series of intricate maneuvers he had done so often before—with sticks. But this time the sword was a real one, and this time his skill was undeniably real too. He fought several men at once, drawing them off, backing slowly toward the edge of the steep mountain slope.

Behind him Willow crawled out from under the corner of the tent, carrying the baby. He watched in wonder as Madmartigan took on one Nockmaar soldier after another, littering the snow with bodies and weapons. Madmartigan saw him staring and bowed with a flourish—"Whoops!"—and slipped on the ice, catching himself just in time. A shield slid past him over the slick surface of the ground. "Willow!" he shouted with sudden inspiration. "Jump on the shield!"

Just then a black broadsword gashed open the tent and Kael climbed through, snarling, "Bowmen! Horses! After them!"

Willow and Madmartigan ran toward the shield, with more soldiers pursuing them. All around them archers took aim. Willow clambered aboard the makeshift sled with Elora Danan. But Madmartigan stopped, looking back as Sorsha emerged from the tent to stand beside Kael. "I didn't betray you, Sorsha!" he shouted. "I love you!"

Arrows rained down on him, and he leaped onto the shield. Sorsha stared after them as they plunged down the mountainside, with Raziel shrieking and flapping over their heads.

"After them!" Kael bellowed. A squad of horsemen

charged down the precarious mountain slope after the sled-shield.

Franjean and Rool crawled out from under the tent. "Where did everybody go?" Franjean asked, looking around in confusion.

Rool shrugged and scratched his head.

Twelve

Willow hugged the baby tightly and crouched between Madmartigan's legs as the shield plummeted down the mountainside, zigzagging through the trees. He looked back and saw the Nockmaar horsemen floundering in the snow that gave the shield such terrifying speed. He gasped as it soared over another snowdrift and thudded down on the other side. Up above Raziel screeched with fright as they sailed on, gaining more speed, barely missing trees and rocks as Madmartigan steered them by shifting his weight. Suddenly Willow's eyes widened. Dead ahead of them was a huge wall of ice.

Willow shut his eyes as the shield sped toward the wall. At the last moment Madmartigan shifted his weight again, steering them into a small crevice. Raziel soared up into the sky, barely missing the wall, and lost sight of them as they disappeared inside the glacier.

They plummeted and swayed downward through a long tube of ice, picking up speed like a toboggan. The tunnel looped suddenly around a full 360 degrees, carrying them with it through a breathtaking moment of upside-down vertigo before it expelled them into daylight. And into the air.

Madmartigan and Willow screamed in terror as the shield shot out over the mountainside like an arrow. But Elora Danan, safe in Willow's arms, laughed in delight. The shield slammed down onto the lower part of the mountain slope, knocking Willow's breath out of him. Behind him he felt Madmartigan lose his grip and fall off. Madmartigan disappeared in the deep snow behind them before Willow could lift a hand. The shield rebounded again and slid on down the mountainside, speeding toward a village he could now see below.

Willow leaned hard to one side as the slope ended, bringing the shield to a halt in a shower of snow just outside the village. "Are you all right, Elora?" he gasped. She cooed, waving her hands. "Everything is going to be fine when you get to Tir Asleen," he said, more to reassure himself than her.

The village children who had gathered around him pointed up the slope, squealing with excitement. He looked around. A huge snowball tumbled toward him, past him, and on into the middle of the village. It crashed to a stop against a building wall, scattering townspeople every whichway.

Willow leaped from the shield with Elora Danan and hurried to join the gaping crowd of villagers. A sword jabbed out through the snowball, chipping away ice, then Madmartigan crawled out, shaking his head.

"Madmartigan!" Willow cried, relieved and furious all at once.

Madmartigan stood up and tried to walk, staggering and blinking. "What happened up there?" he mumbled, looking back up the hill as if he couldn't remember how he'd gotten here.

"You started spouting poetry!" Willow said indignantly.

"I did?" Madmartigan stared at him.

"'I love you Sorsha, I worship you Sorsha'—you almost got us killed!"

Madmartigan gave himself a sharp whack on the side of his head, trying to unscramble his brain. "'I love you Sorsha'?" he said incredulously. "I don't love her. She kicked me in the face. I hate her. . . . Don't I?"

Willow was saved from answering by Raziel's sudden screech overhead. "Kael! Kael!" she cried.

The villagers turned and looked up the mountainside with fear in their eyes. "Nockmaar troops!" someone shouted. They ran toward their houses.

Madmartigan grabbed a passing stranger. "They're after us."

The man nodded. "Come with us." The villagers dragged them in through a cottage door just as Kael's squad thundered into the town.

They were hustled into a dusty storage cellar. As their eyes adjusted, they realized that they were not alone; several other men were already hidden there.

A large hand clamped over Madmartigan's shoulder. "I knew you'd get out of that rat trap," a familiar voice said.

Madmartigan spun around and slammed Airk Thaughbaer up against the wall. "You left me to die, Airk!" he rasped.

"I probably saved your life," Airk said soberly. "We were slaughtered. I lost many brave . . ."

Airk's one surviving captain looked up through the ceiling beams. "Keep quiet!" he hissed.

Madmartigan looked around him at the war-battered men who shared the cellar with him. Most of them were wounded; all of them were exhausted and discouraged. He thought that perhaps Airk had done him a favor after all. Willow held the baby close, shushing her as she began to whimper and more hoofbeats sounded outside.

Perched on a rooftop, Raziel watched as Sorsha joined Kael and his men. "Where is that baby?" Kael demanded. "Sorsha, look everywhere! Pick this village apart!" His men went from house to house, kicking down doors, searching with ruthless thoroughness. Sorsha slid down from her horse. Joining the search with three of her men, she entered the house where Willow and the others waited in hiding.

Madmartigan, Airk, and the rebel captain watched through the ceiling boards as boots pounded the floor overhead, shaking dust down into their eyes. Madmartigan saw Sorsha, not sure what he felt as he looked at her. No one breathed. Willow squeezed the baby against his chest.

Sorsha and her soldiers searched the house but found nothing. They started back toward the door, heading out.

Elora Danan let out a sudden cry. The soldiers stopped dead and drew their swords. But the baby's crying was drowned out by a loud screech as Raziel flapped in through a window and flew madly around the rafters, cawing and shrieking. In the cellar everyone breathed again. Willow put his finger into Elora Danan's mouth to pacify her and sang her a lullaby very quietly.

But as Sorsha started for the door she glanced down and hesitated. She brushed spilled grain aside with her boot and saw the outline of the trapdoor to the cellar. She jerked it open. Outside, Kael rode away with ten men to search along the riverbank.

The rebels crouched down as the cellar door opened, casting a shaft of dusty light across their tense faces. Sorsha descended the stairs cautiously, followed by one of her soldiers.

As she reached the bottom of the stairs, Airk and Madmartigan lunged forward. Airk stabbed the soldier and Madmartigan leaped after Sorsha. She dodged aside, lightning quick, and managed to shout "Down here!" before Madmartigan's knife point reached her throat. The two other soldiers waiting above ran down the steps but stopped short as they looked into the eyes of Airk's rebels. Holding Sorsha hostage, Madmartigan forced them back up the stairs. Elora Danan began to cry in earnest.

"Keep that baby quiet," Airk said impatiently.

"But she needs to be changed," Willow said, climbing the stairs after him. Some things could not be ignored, even in the middle of a war.

The rebels disarmed the Nockmaar soldiers and hurled them into a corner; the air in the room was thick with urgency and fear. Willow changed the baby's diaper rags as quickly as he could while Madmartigan kept watch at the window, guarding Sorsha. "Nockmaar scum," he muttered, watching the soldiers destroy the village outside.

"You'll never defeat us." Sorsha tossed her head. "Give up the baby." She tried to pull free, and Madmartigan clamped his hand over her mouth.

Airk squatted down by Willow, studying the baby.

"What does Bavmorda want with this child anyway?"

"She's a princess," Willow said. "We're taking her to Tir Asleen."

"Tir Asleen?" Airk said. "Nobody's been there in years. Even if you could find it, Peck, she's right—you'd never get past the Nockmaar army."

"There's an even bigger army at Tir Asleen, if we can just get there," Willow answered, not wanting to hear anyone claim otherwise. Airk got up and went to stand beside Madmartigan while Willow rigged a new carrying pack for the baby.

"I've lost more than half my men fighting Bavmorda," Airk said, frowning at Madmartigan. "Now you and this Peck are gonna take her on? You've always said you serve no one, Madmartigan. Since when are you a crusader?" Madmartigan didn't answer.

"He's not going to help you, Peck," Airk said to Willow. "He's a worthless thief."

Madmartigan jerked around. "I'm not a thief, Airk!"

"He's not a thief," Willow said. "Are you?" He broke off, suddenly wondering what Madmartigan really was. Madmartigan looked down, wondering the same thing.

Finally Madmartigan raised his head again. "I serve the Nelwyn, Airk," he said. "Want to join us?"

"You'll never make it, Madmartigan." Airk shook his head.

"Then once again we say good-bye." Madmartigan turned away. The two men began to put on cloaks and armor.

"One day one of us will stand on the other's grave," Airk murmured.

Madmartigan looked up at him. "I hope it's not to-day." He opened the door, pushing Sorsha out ahead of him. Willow followed cautiously. Madmartigan helped Willow and the baby onto a horse, then hauled Sorsha up in front of him on another mount. She struggled and screamed, and the Nockmaar soldiers still searching the town spun around and looked their way.

"Sorsha!" a lieutenant shouted. The soldiers surrounded them, with drawn bows aimed at the escaping prisoners' hearts.

"Weapons down or she's dead," Madmartigan warned. No one moved, but no one fired. "Get going, Willow," he ordered. Willow rode away, looking back over his shoulder. Madmartigan eased his own horse out of town, holding Sorsha in front of him like a shield. When he was out of arrow range he swung his mount around, making it rear up in defiance, and galloped away.

"Get to your horses!" the lieutenant ordered. "After them!" But as he turned back, Airk and his men burst out of hiding to attack the Nockmaar troops. The furious villagers joined them, wielding shovels and spears. One soldier escaped the trap and started after Willow and Madmartigan. "Forget them!" the lieutenant shouted, breaking free and spurring his own horse away. "Get Kael!" They rode off together, leaving the rest of the men to fight a losing battle.

Thirteen

Willow and Madmartigan rode up the ever steepening mountain trails and over a snow-swept pass. Willow kept Elora Danan snug inside his heavy tunic until the road led downward again and the air began to warm. They rode further into the mountains, heading for Tir Asleen.

But the way to Tir Asleen led through the heart of Nockmaar territory; the trail they followed wound below the volcanic peak on which Nockmaar Castle loomed. Sorsha squirmed, looking up at her mother's fortress as they rode through the maze of narrow, twisting canyons. Madmartigan held her tighter as Raziel cawed out directions, flying high above. "This way!" she called. "This way!" The horses pranced and snorted as Raziel led them into a narrow valley.

"Look!" Willow pointed behind them.

"Who's that?" Madmartigan asked, only able to make out a speck on the horizon.

"It's General Kael," Sorsha said. "He's coming for me."

"Well, he's not getting you," Madmartigan muttered. "Or Sticks."

She glared at him. "He's going to enjoy tearing you apart."

"Hurry!" Raziel screeched. "Hurry!"

They edged their horses through the canyon entrance, and went on until the canyon split again into several branches. "To the left! This way!" Raziel ordered.

"It'll be all right, Elora," Willow said, repeating the words for the hundredth time, almost like a prayer. "You must not cry, you must not be afraid. Everything's going to be all right." They rode deeper into the maze of canyons. The way became more difficult, and the horses stumbled and scrambled over the rough terrain. "Willow!" Madmartigan called, almost out of sight behind him. "How's my little Sticks doing?"

"She's asleep," Willow called back. He smiled down at her sweet face as she rested peacefully in the sling against his chest. "You remind me of Mims and Ranon when they were babies. . . ." he said to her. He looked up at the desolate canyon walls closing around him like a trap. "I miss my family. . . ." he murmured to no one.

Behind them Sorsha twisted her body uncomfortably in the cramped saddle she had shared for too long with Madmartigan. "You're holding me too tight," she complained.

"I don't want you to get away," Madmartigan said noncommittally.

"Why? Because I'm your moon?" she asked, her voice thick with sarcasm. "Your sun? Your starlit sky?" She turned her back on him again; her long, heavy hair slapped him in the face.

"Get your hair out of my face or I'll chop it off," Madmartigan snarled. He batted it aside, but it refused to go away. And it was so beautiful . . . and such a nuisance. . . . He grunted with exasperation.

"What are you going to do with me?" Sorsha asked.

"I'm taking you to your father," he said.

She frowned, surprised. "I don't even remember my father. He means nothing to me."

"Raziel says he's a great king."

She glanced back at him again. "You'll never find Tir Asleen," she said. They rode on in silence.

"Did I really say those things?" Madmartigan asked at last.

"You said you loved me," Sorsha murmured, looking straight ahead.

"I don't remember that," he said.

"You lied to me." Her voice took on a sullen note.

"No, I didn't," he insisted, still confused but somehow sure of that much. "I . . . I wasn't myself last night. . . ."

"I suppose my power enchanted you and you were helpless against it?" Sorsha said scornfully.

"Sort of. . . ." Madmartigan shook his head.

"Then what?" She looked back at him, curious in spite of herself.

"It went away," he answered.

"Went away?" she said in disbelief. " 'Without you I dwell in darkness' and it went away?" No one had ever spoken words like those to her; how could he tell her now that it meant nothing? She elbowed him hard in the stomach and slid down from the horse, bolting back along the canyon.

Madmartigan leaped down and scrambled after her,

tackling her in a muddy streambed. They struggled, gasping and cursing, until finally he pinned her down. Breathing hard, they gazed into each other's eyes, both of them suddenly caught in a spell that had nothing to do with magic.

"Hurry!" Raziel cried from high above. "The army! Hurry!" The sound of distant hoofbeats echoed through the canyon. Madmartigan leaped to his feet. He dragged Sorsha up, and she began to kick and hit him again.

"They're coming!" Raziel cawed. "Away!"

As Madmartigan struggled to drag Sorsha back up onto his horse, she punched him hard again and broke away a second time. Furious, he ran after her.

"Madmartigan!" Willow shouted. "Come on!"

"You have no time to lose!" Raziel shrieked.

Madmartigan turned back and swung up onto his horse, letting Sorsha go. But he sat a moment longer, looking back at her where she stood on the rocks, staring at him, while the hoofbeats echoed louder around them. At last he turned and galloped away, leaving her alone in the canyon.

He caught up with Willow just in time for them to pull their horses to a halt. Ahead of them the canyon was blocked by an impassable wall of thorns.

"Raziel!" Willow called. "We'll have to turn back!"

"Light three fires three paces apart and bring down Bavmorda's wall!" Raziel commanded. They leaped from their horses and ran to obey her. Willow held the baby tight, watching for Kael's troops, while Madmartigan urgently chipped sparks into the thorns with a flint.

"Use the fourth chant of unity!" Raziel called to Willow.

"Tuatha luminockt tuatha!" Willow shouted.

"Both of you!" Raziel ordered.

Madmartigan looked up, then looked at Willow. "Me?" he said, incredulous.

"Tuatha luminockt tuatha . . ." Willow began again.

"Tuatha . . . loom—what is it?" Madmartigan demanded.

A flame blazed up suddenly in the wall. "Tuatha luminockt tuatha!" they cried together, perfectly this time. "Tuatha luminockt tuatha!" The wall of thorns burst into flames, withering away as they watched.

By the time Kael and his troops, including Sorsha, reached the wall, there was nothing left of it but smoldering twigs. Willow and Madmartigan were gone.

Fourteen

Willow and Madmartigan galloped out of the maze of canyons and into a lush valley filled with flowers. They pulled their horses to a halt, staring. In the distance stood a beautiful castle gleaming peacefully in the sun.

"Tir Asleen!" Raziel called.

"We're safe!" Willow cried, feeling himself smile at last.

"Come on, hurry!" Madmartigan started on again, looking over his shoulder. He knew they weren't really safe until they were inside the castle's walls.

The gate of the castle stood halfway open, beckoning them in. But as they galloped into its courtyard, Raziel let out an anguished screech. The citizens of Tir Asleen stood frozen all around them, imprisoned inside blocks of foggy crystal by some terrible enchantment. Willow and Madmartigan dismounted and moved cautiously among the frozen people. "Hello!" Madmartigan shouted. "Hello!" An echo was their only answer.

"Oh, Elora," Willow whispered, "this place is awful. I'm sorry. . . ."

Madmartigan turned back to him angrily. "Why'd I listen to you, Peck? 'Everything'll be all right when we get to Tir Asleen.' The only army around here is the one that's about to ride across that valley and wipe us out."

Willow shook his head. "But Cherlindrea said we'd be safe here."

"Safe?" Madmartigan waved his hand at the statues and began to pace back and forth. "Look at these people. The place is cursed, and it's falling apart, and—" He looked down suddenly as his foot landed in something soft and odoriferous. "Trolls?" he said. "I hate trolls!" He wiped his boot on a patch of weeds.

Raziel landed on the crystal block imprisoning a tall, bearded man. "The king!" she exclaimed.

"Sorsha's father?" Madmartigan asked, staring at him curiously.

"This is the work of Bavmorda," Raziel said, flapping her wings. "Willow," she called, "the wand!"

Willow looked up at her. "Are you sure?" he asked. She cawed, tilting her head. They had no choice now but to try. As Willow began to prepare himself for his task Madmartigan moved on, searching for weapons. He disappeared into the castle's armory. Willow began to chant.

"Hurry, Willow!" Raziel urged. "Transform me!"

Willow fumbled, unnerved, and almost dropped the wand. "I can't do it, Raziel. I'm just not a sorcerer."

"But you can be!" Raziel said fiercely. "And you must! Speak—and be one with the words!"

Willow took a deep breath. "Greenan luatha tye thonda peerstaar . . ." he recited, grimacing as pain

98

began to burn along his arm. A sudden noise broke his concentration, and he glanced away, out the castle gates. Kael and his army were thundering toward them across the valley, trampling the flowers underfoot, blowing battle horns, and flashing their weapons. Sorsha rode with them, her long red hair streaming behind her. He stopped chanting.

"Willow!" Raziel screeched.

Willow turned back and gasped in shock. Instead of a raven, Raziel stood before him now in the form of a goat. He took a step toward her, but she bolted away. "Wait, Raziel!" he shouted. "Come back!"

"Willow, you idiot!" Raziel bleated and disappeared among the castle's crumbling walls.

Willow turned away in despair and went looking for Madmartigan. He found him up on the castle wall, readying a catapult. For a moment Willow stopped, not sure that he was really seeing his companion. Madmartigan gleamed in the sun, wearing the golden armor that had belonged to Tir Asleen's king. It was the first time Willow had seen him in something other than rags; the change almost made his wildest claims seem true.

Willow climbed the battlements as Madmartigan looked out over the wall at the approaching army. He glanced back as Willow came up beside him. "Arm that catapult, Willow," he ordered, with the unthinking command of a leader in his voice. He had already set up several booby traps around the courtyard. He ran to the gates, heaved them shut, and bolted them just as Kael's troops reached the walls. Madmartigan grunted in relief, and turned around. He stopped when he found a goat looking at him curiously.

"Good work, Madmartigan," the goat said.

"Raziel?" Madmartigan asked. "What happened to you?"

The goat glanced scornfully at Willow on the battlements. Willow looked down at them and shrugged.

Kael's voice, ordering his men to find wood for a battering ram, reached them from outside the walls. Madmartigan ran back across the courtyard, determined to set up all the defenses he could while there was still time.

Willow followed Madmartigan's orders as best as he was able. He had always been a farmer, never a soldier, but hauling rocks was something every farmer knew about, and so he heaped rocks in piles by every catapult. He searched the crumbling ruins for more ammunition, wandering further and further into the shadowed corners of the castle.

As he reached for a stone, a hideous face suddenly swung down from nowhere and leered at him, hanging upside down with fangs dripping. *A troll!* Willow screamed and ran, bolting across the wooden bridge to the inner keep. He heard the troll start after him. The door at its far end was locked. Trapped there, he looked frantically around. The troll was nowhere in sight, but he could still *smell* it. It was somewhere close by. But where? Willow carefully laid Elora Danan down in a rain gutter.

A battering ram crashed into the gates, making the castle walls reverberate. Willow looked out across the courtyard and saw the gates begin to splinter as it smashed into them again and again. As he watched, the gates crashed open and the Nockmaar army poured through. Madmartigan took aim with his crossbow from the battlements, picking Kael's soldiers off as fast as he could fire.

A huge hairy form swung up onto the bridge; its hands closed around Willow, dragging him back toward its gaping mouth. The troll had found him.

"You're not eating me!" Willow shouted. He punched the troll right in the nose. Startled, the troll dropped him and backed away, growling. But Willow was still trapped. From somewhere below him Raziel called, "Willow! Use the wand!" As the troll lurched toward him again, Willow pulled out Cherlindrea's wand and whacked it on the head. "Avaggdu strockt!" he shouted.

The troll began to disintegrate before his eyes, changing into a blob of fetid, oozing jelly. Wondering what his magic had conjured up this time, Willow kicked the blob off the bridge, hoping no one would notice. It splashed into the moat below, and the water began to bubble and swirl. Willow watched with dread.

Madmartigan fired a catapult filled with spears and arrows, driving back the Nockmaar troops. But they surged inexorably forward again—all of Madmartigan's deadly traps and valiant swordplay only slowed their inevitable advance. Madmartigan gave ground inch by inch as they herded him back toward the moat. Cornered and surrounded, he prepared to go down fighting.

But suddenly the Nockmaar troops stopped, their faces terrified, and began to back away. Madmartigan stared and then grinned. They *were* afraid of him! Then a sound behind him made him turn. He gaped.

An enormous, two-headed Eborsisk rose slowly out of the moat and roared, breathing fire. Willow's transformation of the troll was complete—and far too successful. The Nockmaar troops turned and ran. Not having any other choice, Madmartigan ran with them.

The Eborsisk exhaled fire in all directions, making an inferno of the courtyard. Willow huddled at the end of the bridge, shielding Elora Danan as the center of the bridge burst into flames. At the bridge's far end he saw Madmartigan—trapped with the entire Nockmaar army. Madmartigan looked around frantically and saw Sorsha on the battlements above. She stood frozen, looking back at him. Kael caught sight of him too and roared, "After him!" Madmartigan whirled and ducked into a drain tunnel.

Then one of the Eborsisk's two heads suddenly turned toward Willow. It roared, sending a blast of flames his way. Willow flung himself down, sheltering the baby with his body and expecting instant death. But luck was still with him; a gargoyle deflected the flames. The Eborsisk turned away again to face the attacking army with both its heads.

Willow sat up slowly, surprised that he was still alive. He peered over the bridge at the battle below him . . . and cried out as another pair of huge, hairy hands grabbed him from behind. He spun around and found another troll. He struggled free of its clutches and ran, but there was nothing ahead of him except a wall of flames. The troll loped after him along the bridge, licking its chops.

Madmartigan clambered out of the drainage tunnel's end, firing arrows back down it at the pursuing soldiers. He looked up as he heard Willow's cry and saw Willow and the baby trapped on the bridge. Willow jabbed a flaming stick at the troll, then suddenly reached into his pocket. He flung another magic acorn at the troll—and missed. A second troll dropped down out of the battlements behind him. "Madmartigan, help!" Willow cried.

Madmartigan threw him his broadsword. Willow caught it, lifted it over his head as the troll in front of him started forward—and lost his balance, pitching backward under its weight. The sword came down with a heavy *thud* on the troll in back of him instead, knocking it off the bridge. Madmartigan catapulted onto the bridge and killed the other troll.

In the courtyard below them Sorsha battled the Eborsisk with the rest of Kael's troops, forgetting Madmartigan and everything else—until suddenly she found herself standing by a strangely familiar figure encased in enchanted crystal. Then she recognized her father. She stared as the figure seemed to move, turning toward her. "Sorsha—?" he whispered.

"Father. . . ." she murmured, horrorstruck.

"Sorsha . . ." he gasped, "I'm alive . . . help me . . . help me . . . he-lll-p me. . . ."

Tears filled Sorsha's eyes as she heard his agonized plea. She turned back and looked toward Kael. She watched her mother's general drive his own men to death in a futile battle against the Eborsisk, all because her mother was obsessed with capturing and killing a helpless infant. She looked up at the bridge then and saw Madmartigan, his golden armor shining in the sun as he fought on against impossible odds to protect that child. As she watched, the Eborsisk turned aside from the arrows of the Nockmaar troops to take out its rage on Madmartigan and Willow.

When he saw the Eborsisk turn, Willow ran back along the bridge toward the locked door, carrying the baby. The Eborsisk's hideous heads swung toward them, smoke curling from its nostrils. Madmartigan ran after it and leaped onto its neck. Hanging on with all his strength, he drove his sword through one of the creature's skulls. The Eborsisk swung its wounded head back and forth as it began to swell with unexpelled fire gas. Madmartigan leaped free, falling, and landed heavily on the battlement far below.

As Willow reached the end of the bridge, the locked door suddenly burst open. Nockmaar soldiers crowded through, ready to take the baby from him. "No!" Willow shouted. He swung the heavy broadsword, driving them back. But its momentum dragged him with it, and he tumbled after them down the stairs, landing in a tangle of soldiers. He looked up dizzily. Kael was waiting for him with a malicious smile.

Behind them the Eborsisk's wounded head exploded in a ball of fire; its other head screamed with pain. Nockmaar soldiers surrounded Madmartigan, who lay dazed on the stones below, and raised their swords and spears to finish him. He waited grimly for the final blow to fall. But instead the soldiers around him suddenly began to fall dead at his feet. Madmartigan looked up in disbelief.

Sorsha stood in front of him, her sword still raised. She pressed its tip against his throat, her eyes burning . . . and lowered it again. She reached out, grabbed his wrist, and pulled him to his feet, into her arms. In the middle of the battle's chaos, she gave him a passionate kiss.

And suddenly, as if Fate had changed its mind, two hundred horsemen came charging out of the canyon maze toward Tir Asleen, led by Airk Thaughbaer.

Even Franjean and Rool rode in Airk's saddlebags, brandishing their tiny swords.

The drawbridge crashed down across the moat where the dying Eborsisk lay; Kael rode out, holding Elora Danan high above his head. "Troops!" he shouted. "To Nockmaar! Ride with me!" Stuffing the baby inside his tunic, he charged out of the courtyard with his remaining men.

Madmartigan and Sorsha caught two horses and leaped onto them. "Willow! Willow!" Madmartigan shouted, scanning the melee for his friend. Willow stumbled out of the castle, blood running from his head. "I'm sorry," he gasped. "There were too many of them." Madmartigan swept him up onto his horse and they rode out with Sorsha, following Kael.

Outside the castle walls Kael and his men were battling Airk's army. As Madmartigan reached Airk's side, he saw Kael and four other horsemen escape toward the hills. "Airk!" he shouted. "Kael's got the baby!" Seeing Sorsha, Airk raised his sword. Madmartigan maneuvered his horse between them. "Sorsha rides with me," he said.

Airk stared at him, then at Sorsha, and sheathed his sword. He opened his mouth, but before he could speak the orders came out of his saddlebags. "Warriors!" Franjean barked. "To the canyon!" Rool ordered. The soldiers around them rode away, pursuing Kael's army toward the canyon maze.

Fifteen

Madmartigan and Sorsha led the pursuing rebel troops, driven by their need to save the baby and by a subtle, unspoken rivalry. Madmartigan pulled ahead; Sorsha rode forward to his side again. She aimed her bow and fired, then did it again. Two Nockmaar soldiers fell, struck by her deadly arrows. Madmartigan glanced at her admiringly. He had found a woman he could love at last—and one he could respect as well.

But no matter how hard they drove their horses, they could not close the lead that Kael had on them. Soon Nockmaar Castle loomed into view on the mountain above them. Kael charged toward the castle drawbridge as it began to rise, leaping onto the bridge at the last possible moment. His two remaining horsemen made the jump after him; they missed the bridge's end and tumbled into the dry, rocky moat.

The drawbridge slammed shut with an echoing *klunng*. Madmartigan and Sorsha pulled their horses up short at the brink of the moat. They stared at the castle walls rising above them, huge, dark, powerful—

and evil. "Is there any way in there?" Madmartigan asked.

"No." Sorsha shook her head. "It's protected on all sides." Inside the castle battle alarms sounded. Airk and the rest of his men rode up behind them. Airk looked up at the castle. "We need towers and a battering ram," he said. He turned to his men, shouting, "Make camp! We'll assault tomorrow at dawn!"

The fading sunlight seeped into the vast hall where Bavmorda stood waiting, barely illuminating its dark splendor. Two ancient druid priests hovered nearby. She looked up and watched Kael stride into the room. "What is it, Kael?" she demanded.

He bowed before her. "My queen. I have the child." He pulled Elora Danan out of his cloak; she squirmed and cried as he held her up for the queen's inspection. Seething with hatred, Bavmorda reached out toward the child with hands that trembled with the urge to dash her tiny body onto the hard stone floor. Bavmorda pulled her hands back again. "Good," she hissed. "We will start the ritual immediately! Where is Sorsha?" She glanced past him, looking for her daughter.

"She has turned against us, Your Highness," Kael said.

"Turned against me?" she snarled. In her hate-twisted mind she felt only a burning need for revenge. "I'll deal with that little beast. Purify the altar!" The druids took the crying baby from Kael as Bavmorda stormed out of the room.

The Tir Asleen army pitched its tents on the rugged slope outside the castle and began preparations for the next day's battle. But as they settled in, a presence darker than the night seemed to fall on them like a fog. They looked up in fear. High above them on the castle wall stood Bavmorda, illuminated by the torchlight. The flickering light made the hideous, deformed minions who surrounded her look even more ghastly and terrifying. She looked down at them and laughed. "This is not an army!" she cried.

"Willow! Quick! Hide!" commanded Raziel, still in the form of a goat. She butted him into a tent, out of Bavmorda's view, and followed him inside. "The shelter chant!" she commanded. "Protect yourself!"

"Why?" Willow asked.

"Do it!" she said fiercely.

Willow took the magic wand from beneath his tunic and began to chant.

Outside the tent Madmartigan stood gazing up at the queen. "We've come for Elora Danan!" he shouted. "Turn her over to us!"

Bavmorda laughed. "You dare to challenge me? You are not warriors. You're pigs! Nocklith! Vohkbar! Toa thonna mondarr!" The air crackled with power as she cast her spell over the Tir Asleen army. Madmartigan's body began to contort and change, splitting his armor and transforming into something unspeakably alien.

"You're all pigs!" Bavmorda shrieked. "Kothon lockdar bahkdt!"

Around Madmartigan the rebel soldiers panicked and ran. But there was no escape—one by one their bodies began to expand and contort, ripping out of their armor and clothes. Their weapons and shields fell to the ground, useless.

"Mother! No!!" Sorsha screamed.

108

Bavmorda glared down at her daughter. "You've made your decision," she said coldly. "I warned you never to disobey me."

"Don't do this to us!" Sorsha pleaded. But Bavmorda's finger found her, and she began to mutate like the rest. The mountainside became a sea of writhing flesh as the entire Tir Asleen army was transformed into a herd of swine. Smiling with vengeful satisfaction, Bavmorda wrapped her cloak around her and went back inside.

She climbed endless stairways to the highest, most secret chamber in the castle and threw open its door. Above a sacrificial altar made of shining copper, the druids were binding the crying baby with a leather thong. "Begin the ritual. Now!" she ordered. "Light the first candle."

A druid lit one of thirteen enormous candles that ringed the altar. Bavmorda looked up, glaring at the night sky through the large circular hole in the chamber's roof. "Come, thunder!" she cried. "Come, lightning! Touch this altar with your power!" Lightning flashed in the darkness; she smiled. One druid placed the baby on the altar as the other struck a gong once. "Dark runes, dark powers!" Bavmorda chanted. "Blend and bind, bind and blend, universal night— and the might of Nockmaar!" A gleaming knife appeared suddenly in her hand. Holding it, she grazed her palm and blood welled out. Lightning flashed again, coming closer.

Outside in the Tir Asleen camp, Willow Ufgood was also chanting, his eyes closed in perfect concentration. "Avaggdu luatha bairn off haefermore. . . ."

"It's safe now," Raziel said. "You did well."

Willow opened his eyes and looked around in surprise as he heard strangely familiar grunting noises. He went to the tent entrance, almost afraid to look out. There was no army outside. Amid the tents and fallen weapons, hundreds of pigs wandered . . . and two small piglets, which could only be Franjean and Rool. As he recognized them, the realization of what had happened to the entire Tir Asleen army struck him and he fell to his knees. "I've come all this way and now Elora Danan's going to die!" he cried in despair.

"We can still defeat Bavmorda!" Raziel said fiercely.

He shook his head. "She's too powerful, Raziel."

She stamped the ground with her hoof. "Transform me!" she ordered. "I will destroy her! Hexagram!"

Willow pulled himself together and picked up a sword. He drew a hexagram around Raziel and stepped outside it. He picked up his wand, and began the transformation chant. "Elements of eternity, above and below," he recited. "Balance of essence, fire beget snow." Raziel began to change before his eyes. He struggled to hold on to his concentration, trying not to watch but only to *do*, faltering and regaining his control.

"Don't give up!" Raziel pleaded, her voice as distorted now as her body. "Willow!" she cried as she almost materialized into a grotesque, partly formed creature . . . then into a deer . . . then into a recognizable human form . . . and finally, into herself.

Raziel stood before him in the flesh at last—an aged woman who had clearly been beautiful in her youth, but who had grown old without realizing it, held captive inside Bavmorda's enchantment. Willow covered her unclothed body with a simple smock.

"Raziel!" he called gently, when she did not move.

She looked down at her wrinkled, age-spotted hands. "It's been so long," she murmured.

"I'm sorry." Willow touched her arm.

She looked up at him, her eyes filled with purpose again. She took the wand from his hand. "We've got a lot of work ahead, Willow. We must undo Bavmorda's sorcery."

Willow pulled back the tent flap, and several pigs wandered in. Raziel began the chant that would change them back into warriors.

Three drunken Nockmaar minions glanced up from their bottles at the sound of a baby's scream. They looked toward the queen's tower and away again, muttering. Inside the tower room a druid struck the gong twice as Bavmorda clipped the baby's fine, downy hair and sprinkled it into a Witch's Bottle. "Black fire forever kindled within," she said, "let the second rite begin!" The bottle glowed and sparked, and the heavens answered with distant thunder.

In the darkened camp below, figures—human once again—crouched and hurried from tent to tent. The rebels watched the castle wall with fear in their eyes as Willow and his companions met to discuss a plan of attack.

"We'll never make it inside!" Airk Thaughbaer muttered. "We must return another day."

"Elora Danan will die—" Sorsha protested.

"Upon thirteen tolls of the gong!" Raziel added, reminding them all that there might not be another day.

"Bavmorda is too powerful," one of the soldiers said. Other voices agreed with him.

"She cannot transform you again," Raziel reassured them. "My spell has protected this camp."

"Can you use your magic to get us into the fortress?" Madmartigan asked. Raziel shook her head; the warriors grumbled.

"It's hopeless," Airk said, waving a heavy hand.

"Wait a minute!" Willow, who had been silently listening, suddenly leaped to his feet. "Back in my village we catch a lot of gophers."

Madmartigan grimaced. "Willow, this is war, not agriculture."

"I know, I know!" Willow exclaimed. "But I have an idea about how to get inside the castle. . . ." The others leaned forward, all of them listening now.

A druid struck the gong three times; a third candle was lit. The baby screamed again as Bavmorda's face loomed over her, growing more grotesque with every step in the transferring of power, as the evil forces inside her grew stronger. She dipped her hands into a vat and raised them above her head. Blood ran down her arms into the folds of her black cloak.

"It's too much work to get finished by morning," Airk said when Willow had finished explaining his plan.

"I don't think Kael would fall for it." Sorsha shook her head.

Willow turned to Madmartigan, his last ally. "Please, Madmartigan—Elora Danan needs us."

Madmartigan bit his lip. "I don't know, Willow. The chances aren't good."

"Come on, Madmartigan," Airk said. "You and I are warriors. You know the Peck's plan'll never work." The other soldiers began to mutter again, siding with Airk.

"If the baby dies, all hope for the future is lost," Raziel cried. "I am going to fight."

"Me too." Willow nodded.

Madmartigan raised his arm to silence the protest that tried to drown them out. "Time is running out," he said. "We must decide who's going to leave and who's going to stay. . . ."

Light pulsated inside the queen's tower, high above their camp. The baby lay helpless, streaked with ritual paint, as Bavmorda continued her chanting. "Ocht veth nockthirth bordak! Exile the child to the thirteenth night!" She raised her hand and the baby rose into the air, levitating helplessly above the altar, caught between worlds.

Sixteen

The sun rose on a new day as the gong in Bavmorda's tower rang twelve times. The volcanic slope below Nockmaar Castle lay silent and empty. All traces of the Tir Asleen army had disappeared with the night. Willow and Raziel stood alone on the barren ground among the litter of flattened tents, broken wagons, and discarded shields. The wind howled, swirling bits of debris around them.

"Raziel. . . ." Willow began.

"Willow, I've waited all these years to face Bavmorda," she said, turning to him with a serene smile. "You've made this possible. Whatever happens, I admire you."

Willow looked down again. He took Kiaya's braid from his pocket and looked at it, thinking of home, wondering whether he would ever see his family again, and afraid that he knew the answer.

Raziel glanced at him. "Your son will remember what has happened this day," she said softly.

Up on the wall Kael appeared, answering a guard's call. The guard pointed down at Willow and Raziel standing alone on the silent field below.

"Surrender!" Raziel shouted at Kael.

"We are all-powerful sorcerers!" Willow cried. "Give us the baby or we will destroy you!"

Kael and the soldiers around him roared with laughter. "Kill them!" Kael ordered. The great drawbridge slammed down across the moat with a *thud* that shook the ground. Willow clutched his spear tighter to hide his nervous trembling.

"Patience, Willow," Raziel said.

"Courage, Willow," Willow corrected.

Eight horsemen rode out of the castle, waving their swords. Willow lifted his spear with both hands. He brought it down hard on a war drum that lay in the dust beside him, and its booming voice echoed across the plain.

Madmartigan leaped out of the ground on horseback as all around him the mountainside heaved and buckled, coming alive. Tents and shields flew aside, and the Tir Asleen army charged out of pits and trenches with one loud war cry. They swept over the Nockmaar horsemen and across the drawbridge into the castle. Airk Thaughbaer scooped Willow onto his horse in passing, and Sorsha pulled Raziel onto hers. Together they rode into the castle.

Madmartigan led the assault against the Nockmaar minions who poured out of gates and doorways to defend the fortress. Sorsha slid off her mount with Raziel.

"Sorsha!" Madmartigan shouted. "You are my moon, my sun, my stars!"

Sorsha turned, glaring at him. "Madmartigan—!"

"I mean it," he said. He leaped down from his own horse and gave her a kiss to last a lifetime. Then he swung back into the saddle to join the battle. Sorsha looked after him for a long moment, with her fingers touching her lips. Then she led Willow and Raziel into the labyrinthine heart of the castle.

Slowly they climbed the dark stairs that corkscrewed upward to Bavmorda's tower. Light throbbed behind the door at the top; the sense of the terrifying, uncontrollable power gathering there grew stronger inside Willow with every step he took. A bloodcurdling shriek echoed down the stairwell; the heavy door shuddered and banged as if something monstrous was trying to beat its way out. Willow fell to his knees on the stairs, paralyzed with fear. "I can't go on," he whispered.

Raziel touched his shoulder. "It's all right," she murmured. "You don't have to." He watched the sorceress and Sorsha climb the last few steps to the door together.

Inside the chamber Bavmorda looked up suddenly as the door swung open behind her. The twelve candles around her blew out in a gust of wind. "Raziel . . ." she whispered. She turned to face her challengers; Raziel and Sorsha recoiled when they saw the grotesque transformation already overtaking her. "Good . . ." she hissed, "now you will witness my greatest triumph."

Sorsha stepped forward, her face filled with terror and grief, her hand outstretched. But the sight of her mother's terrible hatred stopped her. "Mother, I . . ."

"Sorsha," her mother sneered, "you're pathetic."

"She has discovered kindness, Bavmorda," Raziel said.

Bavmorda grimaced. "Then you have seen your father."

Sorsha nodded. "Yes, I have. He's alive." Her voice trembled. "I saw what you did to him."

Bavmorda's fury contorted her monstrous face. "Traitor child!" she spat. "I despise you now!" She waved a misshapen hand, and her druids attacked the two women.

Sorsha stepped forward to meet them, defending Raziel, and killed them both with her sword. She hurried to the altar where the baby lay, as pale and silent as if she were dead, trapped in the coils of a spell. "I won't let you kill this child," she said.

"Away!" Bavmorda shrieked. "Avaggu strokt!"

Lightning flashed overhead as Sorsha lunged for the baby. Bavmorda's spell exploded around her, lifting her into the air and sweeping her back across the room toward a wall of spikes. An invisible hand caught Sorsha inches from the spikes, as Raziel's counterspell swept her to safety. Sorsha fell to the floor, unconscious.

"You have gained strength, Raziel," Bavmorda murmured grudgingly.

Raziel drew the wand from her clothing. "I have Cherlindrea's wand."

Bavmorda sent an ax hurtling toward Raziel. Raziel raised her hand, stopping it in mid air. "You cannot defeat our combined power," she answered. She willed the ax back at Bavmorda. Bavmorda raised her fist, and the ax exploded. "Elora Danan will be queen," Raziel said. The air crackled and sparked with clashing energies as the two sorceresses began their final struggle.

Outside in the castle yard another battle to the death still raged. Madmartigan leaped free as his horse was shot out from under him and scrambled to his feet, fighting for his life on foot now. Franjean and Rool scuttled between thudding boots, battling for their own survival. Above them Airk fought his way up the battlements toward a vat of boiling oil. He reached it at last and tipped it down on a phalanx of attacking Nockmaar soldiers. Kael roared a battle cry as he saw Airk and charged toward him with sword and battle-ax swinging.

Back in the tower stairway, Willow found himself moving on up the steps, almost against his will. As he reached the half-open door, it throbbed and blazed with light. He leaped back, tiptoed forward again, and peered inside.

Bavmorda gestured, and the gargoyles on the wall behind Raziel shuddered and came to life.

"There is no one who can match your sorcery, Bavmorda," Raziel said cuttingly. "Except me! Bellanockt!" She spun around, blasting the gargoyles apart with her wand.

"My ritual will negate the prophecy, Raziel," Bavmorda snarled. "The child's energy will be exiled—into oblivion! Strockt!" She hurled a fireball at Raziel, setting her ablaze.

Raziel held out the wand, casting a counterspell that quenched the flames and encased Bavmorda in ice.

Willow tiptoed into the chamber and began creeping toward the baby on silent feet.

"Furrochk . . . Furrochk!" Bavmorda cried. The ice around her shattered, and a sudden storm roared though the room. Willow dodged flying objects and showers of sparks. "Furrochk lithrak!"

A pillar toppled on Raziel, pinning her to the floor. The wand flew from her hand as she fell. She tried desperately to reach it, but it lay just beyond her grasp. Bavmorda came toward her fallen rival, hurling fireballs. Her face was twisted with hatred.

"Hither walha tuatha la . . ." Raziel chanted. The wand whipped into her hand, and she sent a blast of energy toward Bavmorda. Bavmorda flew up to the ceiling, rebounding from rafters and pillars until finally she dropped to the floor. She lay still. Raziel crossed the room to end Bavmorda's evil life.

But as Raziel reached her Bavmorda suddenly sprang to her feet, lunging after the wand. The two sorceresses struggled in a death grip, sending random bolts of energy flying about the room. One bolt struck a chair, turning it into a horrible mutant thing. It staggered away, screeching. Another bolt transformed a table into something that lumbered toward Willow like an enormous beast. He brought one of the ritual candleholders crashing down on it, stopping its hideous progress.

Outside in the courtyard Airk and Kael battled with equal fury on the castle wall while Madmartigan fought off six Nockmaar swordsmen who had him cornered down below. Rool and Franjean scuttled along the parapet, hurling rocks down on their enemies.

Madmartigan looked up when he heard a scream and saw Kael strike down his old friend. "Airk!" Madmartigan cried as Airk tumbled backward down the stairs, mortally wounded. Madmartigan hurled his sword at the last of his opponents, stabbing him in the chest, and ran to where Airk lay. "Airk . . .

Airk!" He knelt, holding Airk's bleeding body.

"If you ever stand on my grave, Madmartigan," Airk gasped, "I'll kill you."

Madmartigan smiled sadly. "Give me your sword, old friend," he whispered, "and I'll win this war for you." He picked up Airk's sword. Airk smiled; then the light went out of his eyes. Madmartigan laid Airk's body gently on the ground. With vengeance shining in his own eyes, he ran up the stairs two at a time, going after Kael.

In the tower above, the private battle of the two sorceresses grew more deadly. Objects smashed and imploded all around them as random energy filled the room. Willow staggered through the whirling chaos toward the altar as Bavmorda struck Raziel and sent her wand flying once more. Bavmorda's twisted hands closed around Raziel's throat to strangle her.

The Tir Asleen rebels fought on, outnumbering and overpowering the Nockmaar army, fighting toward a victory that might only prove meaningless in the end. Madmartigan battled Kael on the wall surrounding the queen's tower, driving his friend's murderer up and back with the fury of his grief. Kael was the best swordsman Madmartigan had ever fought, but Madmartigan attacked like a man possessed. At last he knocked Kael's sword aside and stabbed him through the heart. Kael screeched with rage and toppled over the wall.

In the tower Raziel fell unconscious to the floor as Bavmorda released her. Making his move, Willow grabbed the baby from the altar and ran toward the door. Bavmorda turned at the sound and saw the empty altar. Spinning back, she slammed the door shut with a bolt of energy, trapping Willow and the baby inside. "Bring back that child, Peck!" she roared, in a voice that was no longer human.

Willow turned to face her, trembling. Bavmorda towered over him, a grotesque monster who had once been a human queen, her hands raised to destroy him with her twisted magic. "Who are you?" she hissed.

"I'm Willow Ufgood," Willow said through clenched teeth. "I'm a great sorcerer. Greater than Raziel. Greater than you, even."

Bavmorda laughed. Willow began to walk toward her, reaching surreptitiously into his pocket. He felt the last magic acorn slip into his hand. "I'm the *greatest* sorcerer," he said and threw the acorn.

Her hand flew out, catching it in midair. And then her hand began to petrify. Her wrist, then her arm, turned to stone as the magic crept up her body. Willow backed away, giddy with triumph. But as he watched she focused her dark will on her arm, fighting the acorn's spell, and her arm, her wrist, her hand, turned back into flesh again. She crushed the acorn in her fist and let the dust fall to the floor. "Is that the extent of your powers, little one?" she said scornfully. "Now you will watch me draw upon the energy of the universe to send that child into the netherworld. Place it on the altar."

"No!" Willow said.

"No?!" she echoed, incredulous.

"You stupid hag," Willow cried. "With my magic I'll send her into the . . ." He broke off, groping for a word.

"You're no sorcerer," Bavmorda sneered.

". . . into a realm where evil cannot touch her," Willow finished.

"Impossible!" Bavmorda snapped, intrigued in spite of herself. "There is no such place!"

Willow began to chant. "Helgafel swath ben helgafel, bairn off danu famoww . . ."

"You're a fool," Bavmorda snapped. "I will destroy you and the baby with you. Nyx addanc hogguntt, hoggnutt loatha pox!" She turned away, commanding the wand to come to her. As she turned back, Willow swept his cape in front of the baby . . . and she disappeared.

Bavmorda stared. "Impossible!" she gasped. She staggered backward, stunned with disbelief, and knocked over a sorcery bowl on the edge of the altar. Fluid splashed out, forming a pool around her feet. She screamed, raising the wand. The sky grew bright, lightning bolted through the ceiling and struck her down, and her body contorted and burst into flame. Willow turned away, shutting his eyes as it burned down to a pillar of ash.

Now Raziel began to stir. She raised her head and murmured, "Willow . . . Willow . . . where's Elora Danan?"

Willow bent down to pick up his fallen cloak, with the sleeping baby hidden safely in its secret pocket. His face reddened. "It was just my old disappearing-pig trick," he said modestly. Raziel smiled, pride shining in her eyes. And Willow understood at last that it was not sheer power that made a sorcerer great—it was wisdom. Elora Danan's eyes opened and gazed up at him. Light spilled in through the ceiling, filling the room with the promise of golden days to come.

Epilogue

Bright flags fluttered high above the castle of Tir Asleen, and the valley around it was abloom with flowers. The lost kingdom was alive again with happy activity.

At the castle gate, Willow held the reins of a white pony, waiting to say his final good-byes. The entire court of Tir Asleen had gathered there to see him off. Madmartigan stood proudly beside Sorsha, who held the baby princess Elora Danan in her arms. Sorsha's father, the king, stood at her other side. A trumpet sounded and Raziel came forward from inside the castle, dressed in druid robes and carrying an ancient book. "Willow Ufgood," she said proudly, "take this book of magic. You are on your way to becoming a great sorcerer."

Willow took the book, smiling at the applause all around him. He glanced down at a sudden movement near his feet and saw Franjean and Rool, dressed in uniforms that matched the best Tir Asleen court fin-

123

ery. Neatly trimmed and looking quite civilized, they saluted him with their bright new swords.

Madmartigan and Sorsha came forward with Elora Danan. Madmartigan smiled, the gratitude in his eyes as much for the way Willow had turned his own life around as it was for Willow's part in saving their world. "Good-bye, Peck," he said fondly.

Willow stood on tiptoe for one last look at Elora Danan. She smiled at him too, waving and gurgling. He smiled back at her and gave her a kiss. "Farewell, Elora Danan," he whispered. Madmartigan set him on the pony's back. They shook hands. Then Willow rode away across the valley of flowers, waving good-bye, knowing that the memory of all Tir Asleen waving back at him was something he would carry with him as long as he lived.

He rode home as fast as his pony would take him. But word of his arrival—and his newfound fame—got there ahead of him. As he rode into his village he was surrounded by familiar faces, all greeting his return with wild cheering. Meegosh ran up to him and embraced him, deliriously happy.

"Willow!" a beloved voice called to him above the noise of the crowd.

Willow stood up in his stirrups. "Kiaya!" he called. He leaped from his pony and ran to her. They met in midflight, kissed, and embraced. Ranon and Mims ran up behind their mother, hugging both parents at once until they were swept up into their joyful father's arms.

The High Aldwin came forward, beaming with pride, for he had been proved right in his judgment of Willow's ability after all. Somberly he handed Willow a stone. Willow took it and flung it into the air; it changed into a bird at his touch. The villagers cheered and applauded. Under the smiling heavens, family and friends celebrated the return of their hero with boundless gratitude and love.